Enemy!

Robin Maugham, Viscount Maugham of Hartfield, was born in 1916, only son of Frederic Herbert Maugham, a lawyer who became Lord Chancellor of England in the Neville Chamberlain government. Educated at Eton and Cambridge, he served with distinction with the Inns of Court Regiment during World War II, receiving head injuries which allowed him to convalesce with his famous uncle, W Somerset Maugham. His first major publication was a war memoir, *Come To Dust*. Other publications include *The Servant*, *Line on Ginger/The Intruder*, *The Rough and the Smooth*, *The Black Tent* (all filmed), *The Link*, *The Wrong People* and *The Last Encounter*. He was also author of two books about his uncle: *Somerset and All the Maughams* and *Conversations with Willie*, two volumes of autobiography: *Escape From the Shadows* and *Search for Nirvana*, and several plays. He died in 1981.

Bryan Connon is the author of a widely-acclaimed biography of *Beverley Nichols*. He is currently working on a biography of the Maughams, concentrating on W Somerset and Robin Maugham.

Enemy!

Robin Maugham

New Introduction by
Bryan Connon

Millivres Books
Brighton

First published in 1994 by Millivres Books (Publishers)
33 Bristol Gardens, Brighton BN2 5JR, East Sussex, England

Enemy! first published as *The Deserters* by William Kimber, 1981
Copyright © Peter Burton, 1981, 1994
Copyright Introduction © Bryan Connon, 1994

A CIP catalogue record for this book
is available from the British Library

ISBN 1 873741 18 9

Typeset by Hailsham Typesetting Services, 4-5 Wentworth House,
George Street, Hailsham, East Sussex BN27 1AD

Printed and bound by Biddles Ltd, Walnut Tree House,
Woodbridge Park, Guildford, Surrey GU1 1DA

Distributed in the United Kingdom and Western Europe by
Turnaround Distribution Co-Op Ltd, 27 Horsell Road, London N5 1XL

Distributed in the United States of America by InBook,
140 Commerce Street, East Haven, Connecticut 06512, USA

Distributed in Australia by Stilone Pty Ltd, PO Box 155, Broadway,
NSW 2007, Australia

For
Peter and Ian
With love

Introduction

In the summer of 1942, the German Panzer Division and the Allied Armoured Brigade fought one of the bloodiest actions of the North African Desert Campaign. In the chaos of battle with ground being lost, recaptured and lost again, Lieutenant Robin Maugham, then an intelligence officer, ordered the driver of his scout car on a detour to investigate a burnt-out German tank in the hopes of finding the food containers intact. It was foolhardy because, within minutes, they lost visual contact with their unit which vanished in a sudden swirling sandstorm and, without a two-way radio, they were lost.

By the wrecked tank they found a young German officer unharmed and defiant. Technically, who was whose prisoner was academic, depending on whether they were found by the Germans or by the Allies. To Maugham's relief, it was a British squadron that eventually discovered them. In the meantime, Maugham broke down the German's reserve by talking about his time in Vienna as a student. Suddenly they were not enemies but two ordinary young men chatting nostagically about the days of peace. Maugham mentioned this incident in his first commercially successful book *Come to Dust*, written while he was recuperating from severe battle wounds and, in 1970, he wrote his play *Enemy!* based upon it.

Lord Maugham, as he became, was a popular writer of plays, novels and travel books, best known, perhaps, for *The Servant*, which Harold Pinter adapted for the cinema. His output was erratic in terms of quality and he never emulated the success of his uncle W Somerset Maugham, or escaped from the shadow of his eminent father who became Lord Chancellor in the Chamberlain government before being made a Viscount.

He was bedevilled by his war wounds, suffering intolerable bouts of pain from a sliver of shrapnel lodged so dangerously in his skull that it was inoperable. Early on, he discovered relief in a potent mix of pain killers and alcohol, leading inevitably to dependency. Despite his health problems, later exacerbated by diabetes, he rarely complained and was a popular figure, a generous host and a brilliant raconteur. He was also brave, startling his peers by cheerfully announcing his homosexuality at a time when it was still socially unacceptable. To the chagrin of his famous uncle, who tried to conceal his own true nature from the public, he wrote a series of gay novels of which *The Wrong People* was the most successful.

In what were to be the last two years of his life, his creativity came to an end and it was Peter Burton who suggested a novel based on the encounter in the desert. Maugham was enthusiastic and the result was a collaboration with Burton who had already worked with him on several projects. Although much of the material was recycled from *Come To Dust* and the play *Enemy!*, the book, initially entitled *The Deserters* and published in 1981, was a new work. The sequences which opened out the action and covered the lives of the two young soldiers in London and Berlin were devised and written by Burton.

The strength of the story lies in the development of affection between Rolf and Paul, and the tragic ending illustrates, as Maugham was always concerned to do, the terrible consequences of war.

Bryan Connon

1

The heat during the day was great. It was all a looking forward: in the grey cold of dawn to the sun which must rise to warm chilled bones, in the thirsty heat of noon to the cool of the evening, in the cold loneliness of guard duty to warm blankets and to the final oblivion of sleep.

A strong wind could sweep up clouds of dust from the south. A veil then covered the desert. The wind subsided, and like a moor of purple heather the Western Desert lay serenely in the evening sun.

As the sand ran out slowly through the hour-glass, imperceptibly mind and body changed to endure life in the Western Desert. An invisible stranger in this particular desert square could see that young men from snug little homes in English towns and cities and villages were learning to live in burning heat, and with sand and sores in the desert where man in all things lived candidly with man.

Ten years hence those that survive will have learnt again to depend on the cinema round the corner, water-closets, jazz music and refrigerators, and to be careless of the welfare of the man next door. Tonight in bivouacs dotted round the desert, lean, sunburnt men were drinking their evening brew of tea and preparing to sleep.

In one bivouac, the Sergeant, who had been a miner in civilian life; Ken, the driver, a garage mechanic before the war; Fred, once a commercial traveller but now the tank's gunner; and Michael, the wireless operator, who had been a shop assistant, had settled down for a chat before turning in.

Their bivouac was made from a tank tarpaulin stretched out to form the sides and top of a low tent about three feet high. The sides were supported by wireless poles and a disused lorry hoop placed over a dug-out two or three feet deep, so that they slept below ground level, which kept out the sand. By day one side was left open. They got in at night by crawling under the tarpaulin to avoid showing the light outside, and slept stretched out in one long row. The bivvy was lit by an oil lamp. There was very little room to move. At this moment the men were leaning against their packs, equipment and bed-rolls, which had been unrolled because they would be putting out the lights soon and opening the tent a bit to let out the stale air and tobacco smoke.

The four men were dressed in shorts, boots and puttees; two of them were wearing khaki pullovers; the other two, who had taken them off because they felt too hot, were in their shirts with the sleeves rolled up. Their average age was twenty-two. It would be difficult to distinguish one sunburnt face from another in the smoky light, but their shapes and their voices were well-known to each other.

'Where's our Mr Carey?' Fred asked in his husky voice as he sipped from his mug of tea.

'At a conference,' the Sergeant answered in his deep tone. 'It's for all troop leaders. They're planning an operation in force, as they call it.'

'When?' Fred enquired.

'I don't know.'

'The Sergeant doesn't know. Oh, the Sergeant doesn't know.'

'Smother Fred, will you, someone?' the Sergeant said with a laugh.

'Uncle Rommel is on the move again,' Ken announced. He was a dark-haired, wiry and lithe young man whose frame suggested hidden strength. The set of the lines of his mouth hinted at a sense of humour.

'Bilge,' Michael said quietly, pushing a hank of blond hair from out of his eyes. He was the youngest of the troop.

'Is that petrol filter okay on the tank, Ken?' the Sergeant asked.

'Yes; I fixed it this evening,' Ken answered.

'Then all three of our tanks are on the road.'

'There would be a bloody battle just when we've made the best troop bivvy we ever had,' Fred complained.

'Oh, Fred!'

'You've never been in a battle before, have you, Michael?' the Sergeant asked.

'No.'

'Michael is our new boy. Michael's our virgin to battle,' Fred chanted.

'Let Michael alone,' Ken said. 'He'll be all right. We've all had our first crack at it, haven't we?'

'All right, Ken. Keep your hair on.'

'Fred, you bastard, you've finished all the brew,' Ken said.

'Let's brew up again,' Michael suggested.

'Steady with the water. How much is left in the can?'

'One gallon, Sergeant,' Michael answered.

'That's all right, then.'

'Brew up, brew up, Michael. Put the kettle on,' Fred insisted.

'Put it on yourself.'

'Yes, Fred. Do some work for a change,' Ken laughed.

'Yes, brew up, Fred,' the Sergeant said.

'Nah! There's the thanks I get for all my work.'

'Did you say work?' Ken asked with a grin.

'Who volunteered to do guard last night from two to four?'

'You certainly didn't – you were detailed,' the Sergeant pointed out.

'I wish that Mr Rommel would make up his mind soon. It's about time something happened,' Ken said.

'Ken's itching to get a crack at the Jerries.'

'That I am, Sergeant,' Ken agreed. 'I'll show the bastards. I'm fucking well sick of this fucking desert.'

'Me, too, having to brew up for a lot of sods like you,' Fred mumbled.

'Kick him, somebody.'

'I'd rather be here than at base. You don't get buggered about the place out here,' Ken said.

'That's right, Ken. No spit and fucking polish in the desert.'

'Good old Ken!'

'I'm getting quite fond of the Sergeant out here, aren't you, Fred?'

'Kiss me good-night, Sergeant, dearie.'

'Someone ought to kiss Michael good-night,' Fred said, pointing across at the wireless operator. 'He's almost asleep.'

'I'm all right, really,' Michael insisted.

'What about mixing another drop of tonight's rum issue with the tea? May as well make the best of it, it only comes once in a blue moon,' the Sergeant suggested.

'For heaven's sake don't give Fred any more now,' Ken said. 'His breath smells like a pub already, and I have to sleep next to him.'

'I like that!' Fred exclaimed. 'Anyhow, I don't stink of oil.'

'I work on an engine,' Ken answered quickly. 'You just bugger about with your guns and Michael pansies about with his wireless set going Di Di Di Da Di, Di Di Di Da Di. That's why I smell of oil. And at least *I* don't snore.'

'Heavens, hear him! He snores strength nine clear and undistorted.'

'Stop nattering, Fred, and pour out the brew.'

'I'm always last.'

'That's right.'

'Give him his now.'

'Thank you, Sergeant.'

'When we capture the Italian joy-cart, who'll get his girl last?' Ken enquired.

'Fred will.'

'When they hand out victory medals, who'll get his last?'

'Fred!'

'I'm just unlucky, that's all,' Fred complained.

'You weren't unlucky last time in Alex,' Ken told him. 'I saw you with a swell bit of bint.'

'Fred! You never told your father about that!' the Sergeant stated.

Fred shook his head and gave a sheepish grin.

'I hope you weren't unlucky afterwards,' Ken said, winking at the other men.

'No, I wasn't, see,' Fred protested.

For a moment there was a lull in the conversation. The four men sipped the steaming tea from their tin mugs.

'Who's duty guard tonight?' Michael asked.

'Mr Carey's tank,' the Sergeant replied.

'Thank God for that small mercy,' Fred said. 'We can get a good night's sleep for a change.'

'Turn out the light, someone.'

'Well, here's to the end of another day,' the Sergeant said.

'One day nearer getting back.'

'We're far enough from London now,' Fred muttered.

'Can't believe the place ever existed.'

'Fred, what'll you do when you get home?' Ken asked.

'What'll I do?' Fred said. 'I'll give the old girl a great hug. I'll kiss the kiddies. And then do you know what I'll do?'

'Not arf we don't.'

'Cut it out. You've got a mind like a navvie's hanky. No. It's not time for that yet. I'll go to the kitchen sink and I'll set all the taps running, and then I'll go to the bathroom and hear water running everywhere. Water, water. So much bloody water to drink you could burst with it.'

'Stow it! You make a chap thirsty,' the Sergeant said.

'I'd give a week's pay for a pint of bitter,' Ken announced.

'You've got me all thirsty now,' Michael murmured.

'What about a spot of sleep?'

'Yes. Pipe down now. It's time to get some sleep. Good night, all,' the Sergeant said cheerfully.

'Good night, Sergeant,' Fred answered.

'It's bloody stuffy in here. I'm going out for a breath of fresh air. You coming, Michael?' Ken asked.

'Surely.'

'Draw back the tarpaulin a bit as you go out, will you?'

Fred called. 'And try not to step on my face when you come in again.'

'Good night.'

'Good night.'

Presently the only sound from the bivouac was the steady breathing of the two sleeping men. Outside in the desert, Ken and Michael were talking softly.

'The moon isn't half bright. Look. You can see your shadow.'

'It's awfully quiet, isn't it, Ken?'

Ken nodded reflectively. 'Yes,' he said. 'It's very quiet.' He sighed. 'The desert would be perfect if you could just lay on water and take away the sand.'

'The moon's so bright you can see for miles around.'

Ken laughed. 'Sure,' he said, 'but there's fuck all to see.'

'What are you going to do after the war?' Michael asked.

'I don't rightly know. But I do know one thing. I'm not going back to do sweet F.A.'

'Do you think it'll be like it was after the last war?'

'What, everyone out for hisself again? And no thought for the poor bloody Tommy returning from the fighting? I hope not. It's not much good us fighting if nothing gets done at the end of it,' Ken said fiercely.

'But will they remember that?'

'They must do, this time.'

'The desert is so big it makes you feel awfully small, doesn't it?' Michael said quietly.

Ken nodded. 'Do you feel lonely?'

'Yes – sometimes.'

'Have you got a girl-friend back home?'

'No. I'm waiting till after the war.'

'Michael.'

'Yes?'

'Don't listen to them when they talk about having girls. You don't have to have a girl to be a man! See? And – well, so far as having a friend goes, you've got me. I'll always stand up for you.'

'I can stand up for myself.'

'Course you can. I see you do it. But, I mean, I'll always stand by you – see?'

Michael was silent for a moment, the fine features of his young face set in thoughtful repose. 'Sometimes when they talk about girls they make me sick,' he said softly. 'What do they know about love? They pay for their pleasure and they get it.'

Ken kicked uneasily at the desert sand.

'What's it like?' Michael asked.

'You've never been with a girl?'

'No.'

'Well, don't. Not till you really want to so bad you can't help yourself.'

'There's nothing wrong in it.'

'Not for most, there isn't. It's natural for them. but some people see things different. And if they do, it's bad for them to go after the others.'

'I get worried about it sometimes.'

'Well, don't. You worry about things too much, Michael. That's your trouble. Listen here! I expect you're worrying about this battle?'

'Yes.'

'Nervous?'

'A bit.'

'Well, don't worry yourself. I've watched you on practice runs. You're a good wireless operator, see? I know what I'm talking about, and I tell you you'll be first class when it comes to it.'

'I'll try to be, but ...'

'But what?'

'I could never say this to anyone but you, Ken. I'm frightened.'

'Frightened? Do you think I haven't been frightened? Course I have. I've been so frightened I could feel the sweat dripping down my pants and hear my guts growling. Being frightened doesn't matter. It's what you do that matters.'

'Will I do right?'

'Course you will. Listen. If you get worried, think of me in

the driver's seat right near you in the tank. I'll always be there
to help you – see?'

'I think I'll be all right. You never know before you've been
in action, do you?'

'Listen. I don't often take a liking to someone, kid. I don't
go wasting my love around Cairo and Alex. I've got no girl-
friends there. And I don't love someone that's no good. I know
my instinct. And ... well, I like you, that's all. No. You don't
have to say anything. It's just this stillness and the moon
that's got me.'

'What time is it?' Michael asked.

Ken peered down at the face of his watch. 'Nearly midnight.
What bilge we've been talking! Let's turn in,' he said, turning
back towards the bivouac.

*

'This is it, ahead of us now,' Ken heard the Sergeant's voice
say through his headphones. The tannoy mike crackled but it
worked well and the words were clear.

Suddenly hell broke loose. The quiet stretch of sand was a
torment of shells, bullets, smoke and dust. Simultaneously
tanks appeared from behind the transport and opened up on
them. Then, peering through his visor, Ken realised that
behind the harmless-looking lorries lay concealed big guns;
and the tanks were crawling out towards them. Ken could
smell the smoke and could feel the fat grip of his headphones
on his head. His mouth felt very dry.

'Driver, halt,' Ken heard. He stopped the tank. 'Two-
pounder, six hundred. Traverse right, traverse right. Steady.
On. Jerry tank. Fire.'

The gun recoiled with a deafening crack, followed by a click
as the empty round fell into the deflector bag. The tracer
soared across the desert.

'Right and plus,' Ken heard. 'Same target. Fire. Got it. Got
it. Jolly good. Ken, advance left. Okay. Two-pounder, traverse
right, traverse right. Steady ...'

As the battle raged over the stretch of sand, down in the

front of the Crusader tank Ken was hunched up in his narrow compartment. Headphones clamped tight to his ears so that he could hear the Sergeant's commands down the Tannoy above the roar of the engine. Between his legs were two thick levers. When he pulled the right lever a stream of compressed air pushed out a clutch between the engine and the right track so that the left track churned round faster, and the tank crawled to the right. He was peering through the slit in front of him in the steel wall which surrounded him. The slit was filled with a glass block four inches thick, and through it he could see dimly a narrow strip of sand ahead of him. He was blind on the left side because of the auxiliary turret. Now and then a shell smashed against the armour-plating in front of his body with such force that fittings inside his compartment crashed in on him. He sincerely hoped that if anyone was hit, it wouldn't be himself, because he reckoned that so long as the tank could move there was always hope; but if he was done for, it would be some time before they could get the tank moving again.

In the turret his three friends were pressed close together. The Sergeant stood in the centre with his head half out of the turret so that he could see what was going on around him. If he crouched down into the turret and looked through the commander's periscope his vision was limited and he had to be able to see all round so that he could conform with Mr Carey's movements, who had got to conform with the rest of the squadron. Binoculars, the Tannoy and the wireless mike hung down from straps around his neck. He had to be careful where he put his hands because the two-pounder in front of him recoiled to within six inches of his stomach; he had to keep his hands away from the recoil cage. If the gun's run-out had not been properly maintained it would recoil through his belly. Every man in a tank crew trusted the others with his life.

Michael, the wireless-operator, crouched close to the Sergeant's right thigh and loaded the two-pounder for all he was worth. He flicked in the shells expertly with his right hand so that the rim of the shell pressed back two springs which let the breech-block fly back into position. When the gun was loaded he tapped Fred, the gunner, by crooking his left hand under the recoil cage. All the time he was listening to the wireless and to fire orders. But he knew when the Jerries had got their range by the rocking of the tank and the blast as the shell struck the plating outside. He could not see anything that was going on outside the tank, he could only guess what was happening by listening to the wireless and to fire orders. He stooped to pluck up three two-pounder rounds at a time from the base of the turret, which he could hardly see for the fumes of cordite. He flicked one into the breech, tapped Fred, and balanced the other two on his knees. When these two had been pushed into the black aperture on the gun, he stooped down again.

Fred's forehead was pressed tight against a padded bracket, placed so that his eye could look steadily through the telescope at the small circle of desert to which it was focused. A leather-bound grip was clamped tightly round his left shoulder and under his armpit, and by moving his shoulder up or down he could elevate or depress the gun. His left hand gripped the power-traverse lever. By turning his wrist he could move the turret left or right. His right hand gripped the trigger handles. A tap on his right elbow told him that the guns were loaded. He heard the Sergeant's fire orders on the Tannoy through his headphones: 'Two-pounder.' His hand shifted from the Besa to the two-pounder trigger.

'Six hundred.' He set the range on his telescope.

'Traverse right.' His wrist turned over to the right, and with a hiss of air the turret began to turn around.

'Traverse right.' His wrist turned over more to the right, and the turret screamed round faster.

'Steady.' His wrist turned back a little, and the turret moved very slowly. His eye sought out the target in the small circle of desert it could see through the telescope.

'On.' He could see a tank with its gun pointed towards him.

'Mark III. Jerry tank.' This was the target. He aligned the crosswires of the telescope on the target, aiming off according to range, direction and speed of the tank and the wind.

'Fire.' His right finger squeezed the trigger. The tank was

shaken with a great spasm, and the smell of cordite filled the turret. The tracer soared into his vision and flew up as it struck the German tank.

All four of them were slaves to the gun, shut up in the steel box on tracks which carried the weapon towards the enemy.

Suddenly a great explosion burst in Ken's ears. The tank rocked, and he heard a sharp clatter of metal. The left track had been shot away. Then the Sergeant said, on the air, 'Attack on the left flank. Move left. Move left.'

But the tank couldn't move because its track had been shot away and it wouldn't steer.

'We're getting short of ammunition,' the Sergeant said. 'Slow down the rate of fire.'

'They've got our range, Sergeant,' Ken shouted up at him.

Stuff was crashing against the sides of the tank with such force that the inside fitments were blown against them. It could not be long now. Things looked pretty grim. The tank shuddered again as another shell hit it. The Sergeant's voice said on the air, 'Those of you who can move don't stay there to get shot. Move left. Move left.'

But they couldn't move left because of the damaged track. Ken tried reversing, but the tank began turning round, so that it was almost broadside to the enemy. A shell then jammed the traverse. The Sergeant told Fred to fire whenever a tank came into his line of vision. Ken was frightened now.

Down the Tannoy the Sergeant's voice said, 'Prepare to bale out.'

Fred immediately seized the two-pounder firing mechanism, Besa breech-block and map cases. Michael plucked a valve out of the wireless. The Sergeant seized all the map cases. Ken loosened the flap of metal that protected him. They knew the drill.

The Sergeant's voice said down the Tannoy, 'I'm going to count up to three, and when I say "three" we bale out.'

Ken heard the Sergeant's voice counting 'One, two...' Then a shell landed on the turret of their tank. Ken opened the metal flap in front of him and scrambled out of the tank. He landed softly on the desert sand; he scrambled to his feet and ran round to the turret. His three friends were dead. The shell had been a direct hit and had killed them all. Ken had been lucky.

Now the tank was on fire. It was quite dark, but the darkness was pierced by the red fire of the burning tanks. They crackled as they burned, and the ammunition inside them was exploding. The leading Mark III's opened fire with their light machine guns. Ken still had a chance because they were over six hundred yards away. He scuttled away from the burning tanks and as he ran on he caught sight of a small wadi to his right. He was sobbing for breath. He thought he would never reach the wadi. Then he felt a searing pain in his arm and knew he'd been hit. At last he reached the wadi and flung himself over the edge and slithered down into the soft sand and lay there, too weak to move, waiting for the Germans to come and take him.

But they never came. Perhaps they hadn't time to stop even one tank for the sake of taking one more prisoner. Perhaps they thought they had killed him when he fell down. At any rate they never came.

As soon as he had got his breath, Ken scrambled into some camel-grass and concealed himself as best he could. Then he examined his wound. At that moment it didn't look very serious, though it was painful. The bullet had ripped across the top of his forearm. The gash was bleeding, but it was only a surface wound. He bound it up with his field-dressing.

Somehow Ken had broken his watch. But it was no more than half an hour after he had reached the wadi that the sandstorm began. The south wind was now sweeping up the sand into a thick cloud which covered the desert like a cloak. Ken had taken his shirt off and wrapped it around his mouth and nose so as to prevent sand clogging the orifices. He panted for breath in the sultry heat and kept his eyes screwed tightly closed. The sand whipped against his sweaty clammy body, stinging him sharply. As he lay in the roar of the wind and the whirling sand, Ken made his plan.

Rommel's attack was moving north and east. His side was withdrawing eastward. Therefore if he moved to the north or to the east he would risk running into enemy troops. His only chance was to go south and hope he would be able to skirt round to the east when he had got out of the battle area. Perhaps his choice was wrong. Perhaps it would have been better to make for the coast. Anyhow, once he'd made the decision, he'd stick to it.

There was only one snag. Although he'd got a compass, he had no food and, far worse, no water. His only hope was to find a stray tin. Often odd tins of food or water were lost or abandoned in the battle area.

Though the storm was still raging when night closed around him, Ken decided to begin plodding south. He buttoned himself back into his army shirt – though it was little enough protection against the chill desert night – and tied his handkerchief over his mouth and nose and started walking. He held his compass in front of him and moved slowly south.

Towards dawn the storm lifted, and the sun's rays stretched out to warm the sands of the desert. As the sun rose higher in the sky, the heat became more intense but he still forced himself to walk on, hoping to find food or water. Presently he saw something black, lying in the sand ahead of him. He quickened his pace. As he came nearer he saw it was a jerry-can. Hurriedly he stooped and picked up the can and shook it. The can was empty. Disgustedly he threw it into the sand, then savagely kicked it so that it bounded away down the tumbling sand of the dune. He walked on.

In the next clump of coarse camel-grass, he lay down and tried to sleep, but his arm was throbbing and he was horribly thirsty. The sun rose inexorably hotter and hotter. He covered his head and forced himself not to think of water and all cool things – but his imagination was stronger than his will-power and clear-edged images of mountain streams, glaciers, water-meadows, ice clinking in misty glasses, and most of all, of foaming pints of bitter as served in his local back home in England filled his mind's eye.

Though he dozed a little, he kept waking up to find the sun beating down on him. The heat was intense and he knew there could be no escape from it, no way of avoiding the burning rays, until it began to go down. His throat was parched, and though he kept drifting into a fitful sleep he didn't awake refreshed. The day seemed endless and the progress of the sun across the sky seemed to be slower than the pace of a garden snail. But, at last, it began to set.

When it was cooler, Ken began walking again. By this time he was weak and exhausted, hungry and thirsty. He no longer feared capture; capture would come as a blessed relief from the stark and lonely horrors of the empty desert. He stumbled through the first hours of the night until he could go no further. He decided to lie down for a short rest in an attempt to conserve such energy and strength as remained with him.

When he awoke, the sun was again rising in the sky. It was already hot. His wound was throbbing and his thirst was anguish. For a time he lay hopelessly still. In despair he felt that there was no point in moving; it would be as easy to stay where he was. Maybe it would be easier to die than to struggle grimly on through the dead landscape. But the instant of total despair passed. With a tremendous effort of will, Ken dragged himself to his feet. His eyes searched the horizon in the hope of seeing some indication of life or shelter or water or food. But nothing stirred; there was no sign of life – not even so much as a scavenging bird disturbed the clear blue of the sky.

He knew that he must move to find water soon, because he was certain that he could not endure the scorching heat of another day. Slowly Ken began to move forward, step after agonising step, dragging himself across the burning desert sands which stretched infinitely before him. No longer did he look round for fear of being spotted by the enemy. Frantically, at every moment, he scanned the horizon for a speck that might reveal a human being who could give him water – a human being, friend or foe.

As the sun rose higher in the sky he began to panic. Wild thoughts shot through his mind. Was he going north rather than south? Perhaps he was heading for a vast and endless empty space? He paused for a moment and stared down at his compass. He was heading south.

Then to the west he saw what in the shimmering heat

looked like a ramshackle hut perched on the horizon. He stumbled feverishly towards it, fearing it might be a cruel mirage. At that instant, he fell. For a while he lay motionless, gasping for breath – for the fall seemed to have completely winded him. As he slowly regained his composure, he forced himself to stand. Slowly he edged himself closer towards the hut. His weakened and tired state caused his legs to tremble; he realised that he was afraid.

The fear left him as he drew closer to the shape in front of him and through the glare of the sun he was able to focus his eyes more clearly on it. Ken realised that it was not a hut which he was staring at; he saw it was a derelict English Crusader tank.

As he moved, Ken realised that the hand which had held the compass was empty. He stopped. He must have dropped it in the sand when he fell. He turned and stared back at his tracks in the gently shifting sand. Already the slight breeze was causing the grains of sand to blow back into the footprints. Wearily he moved back along the way he had come. He knew he had to find the compass – for without it he could wander in circles in the desert. A heavy indentation in the sand indicated the spot where he had fallen. He hastened forward, attracted by the sun glinting on the glass of the compass as it lay in the sand. A sense of relief surged through his body. He had found it. He stooped down. As he scooped the compass from the sand, he saw, to his horror, that it had broken as he fell. A sense of despair gripped him. He cursed and threw the broken instrument back to the ground. Angrily he kicked it away from him and watched as it bounced down the dune and out of sight.

He turned and began to trudge back towards the derelict tank. At least there was a chance it might still have food and water on board.

As he approached the Crusader tank he saw that the gun was twisted from the shattered turret and the tracks lay rusted and broken flat on the sand. As he drew nearer, he observed away to the east the shape of two graves in the sand with roughly made wooden crosses jutting from the mounds. He continued to walk forward towards the tank. Around it was a litter of equipment – empty tins, jerry-cans, a battered canvas chair.

To the right of the tank was the carcass of a trailer over which was stretched a camouflage netting and a tarpaulin forming a bivouac. Beyond it was the clear blue sky and the harsh reality of the endless desert stretching away as far as he could see. Suddenly the afternoon seemed just pleasantly warm. The discovery of the wrecked tank had given him hope and, in some strange kind of way, had taken the sting from the rays of the sun.

As his eyes searched the sand around the tank, Ken spotted a water-bottle. He moved towards it and threw himself down in the sand beside it. He lifted the bottle carefully and shook it. A smile stretched across his face. The bottle was at least half full. He felt the horror of the last days and hours lifting as his spirits rose. Water! He wrenched the bottle open and raised it to his lips. The warm water trickled down into his mouth and slid down his parched throat. At that moment the water tasted finer than anything he could think of – it was as stimulating as a pint of best bitter in his local, more exciting than a stiff whisky chaser. As the water filled his stomach, he felt a different person.

2

After Ken had drunk all the water, he replaced the cork and put the bottle back in the sand. He wiped the back of a hand across his wet lips, then relaxed and looked around him. He stared at the markings of the tank, noting the paint was flaking in the sweltering heat.

Ken could feel the grains of sand sticking to his sweaty damp flesh. He pulled himself to his feet and brushed away the sand which had covered the backs of his legs. His bush shirt was clinging to his back and was ringed with dark patches of perspiration beneath the arms. His black curly hair was tangled and matted with sand. His beard was a scruffy dark stubble which irritated and rasped as he rubbed a hand across his chin.

He stared towards the bivouac; then he approached it more closely. The tarpaulin caused the sand beneath it to be in heavy shadow – but Ken had observed a figure lying on the sand, sprawled on top of a wide sleeping bag. Cautiously, Ken edged closer. Something about the still figure made him feel sure that it was not a corpse. Ken crouched down on his haunches and peered under the flap of the tarpaulin. At first the change from the blinding light of the sun to the dimness of the shelter caused him to have difficulty in seeing, but soon his eyes adjusted and he was able to see clearly the figure on the sleeping bag. Ken stared down at the carelessly sprawled limbs and slender form of a young man, not even as old as himself, he suspected, probably no more than about twenty-one or two. Strands of hair so blond that it might almost have been white flopped over the youth's forehead, making his appearance seem especially boyish. The faintest of blond fuzz showed on his face, suggesting that he had little need to shave very often. The young man was dressed in shorts, otherwise he was naked. His skin was sunburnt and smooth and against the brown of his flesh gleamed a thin silver chain from which hung a small identity disc. A small trickle of saliva appeared at the corner of the youth's mouth. He grunted and moved restlessly in his sleep, but he showed no sign of awakening.

Ken kicked the young man's foot. 'Wakee, wakee. Rise and shine,' he said. 'You've got company.'

The young man opened his eyes and blinked. For a moment his eyes closed again, then they opened and stared up at Ken. There was an expression of bewilderment on the young man's face. Suddenly, as he came fully awake, the young man stiffened.

'Awake at last, are we?' Ken said, smiling. As he spoke, he noticed another water-bottle lying near to the young man. He picked up the bottle and sat down. 'Full,' he said. 'Full. Would you believe it! I've stumbled into a bloody oasis. Can you spare it?'

The young man remained silent.

'You've got to spare it, mate,' Ken said. 'I've been without water for two horrible days.'

Ken lifted the bottle to his lips and began to drink thirstily from it. As he greedily gulped down water, a thin trickle ran down his chin and splashed onto his shirt.

'Cor, that's better,' Ken said, beaming towards the young man.

Slowly the youth was sitting upright. He glared angrily at Ken.

'It's all right,' Ken said. 'I won't take any more than my share.'

The young man stared silently at Ken. Then he scrambled to his knees and crawled out of the shelter of the bivouac. Once outside, he struggled to his feet and brushed the sand from his legs.

Ken finished drinking. He replaced the cork in the bottle and stood it carefully in the sand beside him. He leaned forward and fumbled with the laces of his boots, untying them. He eased the boots from his feet with a groan of pleasure. He held one boot in the air and let the sand within it trickle out. Then he stood the boots neatly next to the water-bottle.

'See,' Ken said, looking up at the young man. 'I didn't drink no more than my share.'

The young man scowled and began to move away around the tank.

By now Ken had his back to the young man. 'You're a strange one,' he said, smoothing the sand in front of him with the palm of his hand. 'What are you up to now?'

The young man climbed up on to the body of the tank. He gazed away towards the horizon. The sound of Ken's voice drifted up to him. With a shrug of irritation, he turned and stood for a moment glaring down at Ken. An expression of fury crossed the young man's face. He shook his head as if in disbelief and jumped neatly from the tank. He landed with a soft thud in the sand. He fumbled with a lid on the side of the tank, opening up a compartment.

'How long have you been here?' Ken asked. 'When did this lot brew up, then? Last week's patrol? What's your unit?'

The young man remained silent, slowly turning back towards Ken.

'Now what's wrong with you, cock?' Ken asked. 'Lost your voice? Shock or something? Or don't you take to my face? For Christ's sake – say something – if it's only to tell me to fuck off.'

The young man was moving back towards Ken. In his hand was an army revolver – and the barrel was pointing towards Ken.

Something about the young man's silence struck Ken as ominous. He turned his head. 'Trust me,' Ken said, staring at the revolver. 'Trust my fucking luck. Lost for two days in this God-forsaken wilderness without seeing a blessed thing. Then I spot a tank. A Crusader tank – one of ours, mind. And blow me if the bloke that's asleep beside it doesn't turn out to be a Kraut ... Where's the rest of your crew?'

The young man's voice was harsh and hostile. 'Over there,' he said in English, nodding his head towards the horizon. His voice had only the slightest trace of an accent.

'Oh. So you speak English, do you?' Ken asked.

The German ignored Ken's question. 'Stand!' he said in a voice of command.

Ken heaved himself to his feet.

The German moved closer to him, knocking a canvas collapsible chair out of the way as he approached.

'All right,' Ken said. 'Don't get excited.'

'I am not excited,' the German announced stiffly. 'But I am taking you prisoner.'

The German moved forward and ran his hands quickly over Ken's body, checking to see if he was carrying any weapons. He stepped briskly back.

'Where's your gun?' the German asked.

'Back in my tank,' Ken answered. 'Brewed up with the rest of it.'

'You are alone?' the German asked.

'Looks like it, doesn't it?' Ken said, grinning.

The German's expression remained stern and humourless. 'I ask you – are you alone?'

'Yes,' Ken replied wearily. 'I am alone.'

'*Gut*,' the German said with a nod. 'Now. Your name, rank and number?'

'Preston. Trooper. 1293276.'

'Your regiment?'

'I don't have to answer that,' Ken announced. 'I only have to tell you my name, rank and number.'

The German was silent for a moment. His gentian blue eyes were without expression. 'You were in tanks?' he asked.

'I don't have to answer that one either,' Ken said. 'But since I don't suppose it'll help Hitler to win the war, much. Yes.'

'Where are the rest of your crew?'

'Dead ... Where are yours?'

The German inclined his head. 'Back there,' he said.

Ken turned around and scanned the desert carefully. 'No, they're not,' he said.

'Yes,' the German insisted. 'They are below the ridge.'

Ken glanced at the tank. 'So this is one of the Crusaders you Jerries captured in the winter campaign?'

'Yes. *Bestimmt.*'

'When did it brew up?' Ken asked.

The German did not reply.

Realising that the German had not understood the question, Ken rephrased it. 'When was the tank destroyed?' he asked.

'Last week.'

'No it wasn't,' Ken said. 'This tank hasn't seen action for at least a month. Look at the tracks. They're quite rusty ... I don't believe you fought in this tank ... And I don't believe your crew are below that ridge.'

The German levelled his revolver at Ken. 'Stand!' he snapped.

'You can't shoot a prisoner,' Ken said. 'I thought every one of Rommel's soldiers knew that.'

'You *can* shoot – if a prisoner tries to escape.'

'Yes. But I'm not trying to escape. Besides – where is there to escape to?'

Unexpectedly Ken leapt on to the tank.

'Stop!' the German demanded. 'Stand!'

Ken ignored him. He peered into the shattered turret of the tank. He recoiled in disgust.

'There must have been two men in that turret,' Ken muttered. He stared grimly at the German. For a moment there was silence.

'I found two graves below the ridge,' the German said.

'And the rest of the crew?' Ken asked. 'The other two?'

'I don't know,' the German answered.

'You don't know!' Ken shouted and flung himself from the tank at the German. The two bodies collided with a violent thump. The revolver was knocked from the German's hand. The German stumbled and tried to shake Ken from his back. They stumbled and fell heavily. For a while they rolled about

in the sand, clutching at each other, punching and kicking.
Then they staggered to their feet. The German made a move
towards the gun, but quickly Ken dived for his legs and sent
him sprawling, winded, in the sand. Ken reached for the
revolver and pointed it at the prone German.

The German rolled over on to his back and lay staring up at
Ken with a look of hatred. Suddenly he sprang up and
snatched up a shovel which rested against the side of the tank.
He raised it above his head and charged towards Ken.

'Drop it! You murdering bastard,' Ken said in a steely
voice. 'Drop it. You killed them. You crept up at night and
killed them, didn't you?'

Ken aimed the revolver at the German.

A look of shock passed across the German's face. 'No,' he
muttered, shaking his head. 'No.' Dejectedly he let the shovel
fall to the ground.

'Yes,' Ken shouted. '*You* killed them. This tank wasn't
captured in the winter campaign. It's the new model
Crusader. Its crew weren't Jerries. They were English,
weren't they? Weren't they?'

The German nodded. 'Yes,' he said quietly. 'They were
English.'

Ken shuddered. 'And you killed them,' he said. 'It's all
dried up now. But it's blood in that turret. All round it. You
killed them.'

'No, no. I never saw the men of the crew,' the German said.
'The tank was already abandoned when I found it.'

'Liar. You said the rest of your crew were below the ridge.
But they're not, are they?'

'No.'

'You're alone here?'

'Yes.'

'How come?'

'Why should I tell you?'

Ken moved forward and sharply prodded the German's
stomach with the gun.

Ken grinned. 'Because *I've* got the gun, now see,' he

declared. 'Now, you tell me ... Your name, rank and number?'

'Paul Seidler ... *Gemeiner Panzersoldat* ... *Zweihundertfünfund-vierzig. Acht vier sechs sieben.*'

'*Heil Hitler!*'

Paul Seidler glared at Ken. '*Bestimmt. Heil Hitler,*' he answered.

'Twenty-first Panzer Division?' Ken asked.

'*Jawohl.*'

'Tank crew?'

'Yes.'

'What?'

The German looked confused. 'What do you mean?' he asked.

'What place in the tank?' Ken said.

'Gunner.'

'What kind of tank?'

'Mark Three.'

For a moment there was silence. Ken was watching the German's face.

'It's all dried up now. But it's blood in that turret. There's blood everywhere,' Ken stated.

'Yes.'

Ken stared at Seidler. 'But the turret hasn't been penetrated from the side,' he said coldly.

'I know,' the German answered. 'But look again. You'll see that the shell landed from above. The tank may have been stopped from the ground. But it was knocked out from the air.'

Ken turned away and moved towards the canvas chair lying on the sand. He picked up the chair and set it upright. He sat down, still covering Seidler with the revolver. The German had his hands placed on top of his head.

'Your division's up north by Gazala – at least it was four days ago,' Ken said. 'What are you doing down here?'

Seidler slowly lowered his arms until they were resting by his sides. 'Our troop was sent down south on patrol,' he answered. 'We ran into a force of British tanks. Two of our

Mark Threes escaped. But our Sergeant's tank – the tank I was in – got stuck in soft sand.'

The German stopped speaking for a moment and gazed across at Ken.

'Yes?'

'Our Sergeant gave the order to abandon tank and run for it,' Seidler continued. 'When I jumped out of the turret, I fell. That saved me, I think. Because the others were killed by machine gun fire.'

Once again the German stopped speaking. His hands moved restlessly at his sides.

'Go on,' Ken prompted.

'But I lay down in the soft sand ...' Seidler said slowly, his voice trembling. 'The bullets were coming over me ... It was late in the day. Before the Crusaders returned to my tank I had got away into the darkness.'

Ken nodded his head. The young German's experience was not so very different from his own. He could feel the rigid hostility draining from him.

'When was that?' Ken asked.

'Five nights ago ... For two days I walked looking for our lines, of course,' Seidler said. He was now speaking very slowly, as if trying to remember some incident from long past. 'Then I saw this tank,' he continued. '*Es war fabelhaft*. The cans of water are still full. There are tins of biscuits and tins of meat. So I decided I should stay here. At least I have food and water and shelter and a warm bed to lie in at night. I think the bed must have belonged to an officer ... Soon, when we advance again, they will find me. And I shall be safe.'

'What makes you so sure that Rommel *will* advance?' Ken enquired.

'It is certain,' Seidler replied flatly. 'Within a month we shall take Tobruk. Within two months we shall be in Cairo.'

Ken smiled at the German. 'You won't even get as far as Tobruk,' he said.

The young German proudly raised his head. 'You cannot stop us,' he announced firmly. 'Nothing can.'

'Bollocks.'

'Wait and see.'

Ken smiled again. 'Tell me something,' he said. 'How come you speak English so well?'

'Well, I studied English at school,' Seidler answered. 'So I had the groundings of it already. And then I have lived in England for two years before the war.'

'Doing what?' Ken asked, glancing at him in surprise.

'I was in England to study the hotel business,' the German answered, speaking very slowly. 'My father is the manager of a hotel in the country near to Berlin.'

'Free nosh and booze, I suppose, Paul,' Ken said with a friendly laugh. 'It's all right for some.'

Paul stared at Ken without comprehension.

'Free food and free drink,' Ken explained. He stood up.

Paul gave a small smile. 'Sometimes,' he said.

Ken began to walk around the tank, whistling softly to himself. 'Speaking of food and drink,' he said, 'where are all these tins you were talking about? I'm starving.'

'There are some in the bivouac,' Paul told him.

'Then get some out,' Ken said. 'Chop, chop. I'm so hungry I could eat a horse.'

'Get them yourself,' Paul replied. But he shrugged his shoulders and walked over to the bivouac to find some tins of food. He disappeared into the shelter of the bivouac.

As soon as Paul was out of sight, Ken hastily opened the chamber of the revolver and emptied the bullets into his hand. He snapped the gun shut and slipped the bullets into the pocket of his shorts.

'Here,' Paul said, crawling out of the bivouac, dragging a rucksack which he deposited at Ken's feet. 'Food.'

Ken peered inside the canvas bag. 'Christ!' he exclaimed. 'There's enough grub here to last for a week.'

'Eat, then,' Paul said. 'Help yourself.'

Dropping the gun on the sand, Ken dug into the rucksack and pulled out a tin of bully-beef. Fitting the key to the tin, Ken began to open it.

Paul watched Ken intently. As Ken started to tug the meat from the tin, Paul quickly moved forward and snatched the revolver from the sand.

'Stand!' Paul cried out.

'Eh!'

'Put down that tin.'

'Why?' Ken asked, stuffing bully beef into his mouth.

'You are my prisoner,' Paul said, speaking in a firm voice. 'You will eat when I say you can.'

'Bollocks.'

'Put it down,' Paul repeated.

'You can't make me,' Ken said, breaking off another piece of meat and stuffing it into his mouth.

'But I can,' Paul announced, aiming the revolver at Ken. 'But I can make you ... most easily.'

'You can't shoot your prisoner while he's having his afternoon grub,' Ken told him, chewing his mouthful of food. 'It says so in the Geneva Convention.'

'I might get so angry I would forget the Convention,' Paul declared.

'You might,' Ken conceded. 'But it wouldn't do you any good.'

'Nor you – not with a bullet in your middle.'

'I wouldn't be too sure about that bullet, old cock,' Ken said and winked.

With growing understanding Paul nodded. He broke open the chamber of the revolver and peered inside. Ken grinned up at him and continued to eat. Paul glowered down at him.

'You are still my prisoner,' Paul said.

'All right,' Ken nodded in agreement. 'I'll promise to be your prisoner all day. Will that please you?'

'And tonight also,' Paul insisted.

Ken shook his head. 'No, I can't be your prisoner tonight,' he said.

'Why not?'

'While I was asleep you might cut my knackers off.'

Paul stared at Ken in astonishment. Then Ken looked up at Paul. He wiped grease from his lips with the back of his hand.

He gave a broad wink. For the first time Paul really smiled.
Suddenly the smile turned into laughter. The tension left his
face and he looked very young and almost happy.

Ken grinned at Paul. 'Be a good boy and get your prisoner a
knife or a fork,' he asked, 'I'm getting my fingers all greasy.'

Paul vanished into the bivouac for a brief moment; when he
reappeared he threw a fork across to Ken.

'Thank you,' Ken said, retrieving the fork from the sand.

'Give me a tin,' Paul requested.

'Sure,' Ken said, taking a second tin from the rucksack and
tossing it across to Paul.

'*Danke* ...' Paul said and threw a plate across to Ken.

'*Danke*!' Ken said promptly and laughed. 'We're like a
bloody juggling act at the circus.'

'Biscuits?' Paul asked.

Ken nodded. 'Good old army biscuits,' he said. 'As solid as
the Rock of Gibraltar ... and twice as hard.'

'I like them,' Paul stated.

'You can have 'em,' Ken said throwing the biscuit tin to
Paul. 'What else have you found in the tank?' he asked.

'Army clothes,' Paul replied. 'Full equipment nearly.'

'What do you think happened to the crew?' Ken asked.

For a while Paul was silent. 'Two were killed when the
turret was hit,' he began. 'The other two got out alive, I think.
Perhaps it was they who buried their friends.'

'I saw the two graves as I arrived here ...' Ken told him.
'Poor buggers. That's why the turret is in such a mess. I don't
know which is worse – being shot up from the air or being
shelled ... Our tank was hit by a shell, and that was the end
of it.'

'But you were in the tank,' Paul said.

'The shell landed on the turret,' Ken explained. 'I'm a
driver. I was right down there in the driver's seat. I wasn't
even grazed. The three of them in the turret ...' Ken looked
down at the sand in silence. 'At least it must have been quick.
When I got out there were still some Mark Fours milling
around to the north. I was hit by a bullet, but I managed to
keep going. I headed south for a bit. I intended to go south

and then head back east ... but then I fell and my compass broke. Luckily I was in sight of this tank. But really I've been lost for two days ... When I woke up this morning and looked around ... I saw nothing but desert ... nothing but bleedin' desert for miles and miles around. Not a sign of life. Not so much as a lizard to keep me company ... I thought I'd had it.'

Ken stopped speaking. He nodded his head and managed to smile wryly at Paul. When he began to speak again the tone of his voice had changed completely.

'This stretch of desert, I thought to myself, will see the end of Kenneth George Preston of number eleven Oakridge Road, Fulham,' Ken said and sniffed loudly. 'It was a nasty moment, I don't mind telling you ... I could even see the obituary notice in the local paper – with a black border all round it.'

Ken held up a hand solemnly. ' "He died without an enemy in all the world",' he quoted as if reading from a newspaper. 'Except for the bleedin' Jerries, that is, saving your presence ... "He will be mourned by his many friends in Fulham" – not to mention Hammersmith and Putney – "lamented by his comrades in the Hartland Yeomanry" – there now, I've told you the name of my regiment and helped Hitler win the war – "lamented by his comrades in arms" – except perhaps for the RSM and that bastard Captain Baldock ... "The world will be a poorer place without Ken Preston. A poorer place without him." '

Ken looked across at Paul and smiled. A strand of hair had fallen down over Paul's forehead, but he seemed oblivious of it as he listened to Ken speaking.

'And so it would have been a poorer place,' Ken stated. 'But as it is ... well, you can pass me that water-bottle.'

Ken placed the tin plate and fork on the sand. He leant his head back against the canvas chair. Paul watched Ken for an instant, not wishing to disturb the other man. Then he picked up the water-bottle, stood up and carried it over to Ken.

'*Danke*,' Ken said softly.

Paul reached into the pocket of his shorts and extracted a packet of cigarettes. He extended the packet towards Ken. 'Cigarette?' he enquired.

Ken took a cigarette from the packet. 'Cigarette!' Ken exclaimed. 'Christ! What is this? The fucking Ritz Hotel? How many have we got?'

Paul took a cigarette for himself and replaced the packet in his pocket, *I* have got five packets,' he answered.

'Which you nicked off this tank,' Ken announced.

'Which I removed from this tank when I found it here and captured it,' Paul stated.

'So now you've captured the tank,' Ken said ironically.

'I have captured the tank,' Paul told him, 'and I have captured you.'

'What a bloody lie!' Ken exclaimed.

'You are my prisoner,' Paul insisted with a gentle smile. He flicked at a lighter and lit Ken's cigarette, then his own.

Ken sucked in smoke, then exhaled luxuriously. 'Only till tonight, mate. Remember,' he reminded Paul. 'Tonight I may escape. Or I may take *you* prisoner. I haven't decided yet. It depends on how the mood takes me.'

'You won't leave this tank. And you know so,' Paul said firmly.

'Don't be too sure,' Ken replied. 'I might even take you with me. At pistol-point, of course.'

'Bollicks!' Paul said, and sat down on an up-turned ammunition box.

Ken laughed. 'Well, fuck me. I never thought I'd hear a Kraut say that. But it's not bollicks, it's bollocks.'

'Bollocks,' Paul repeated.

'And the same to you,' Ken muttered. 'Where do you live in Krautland?'

Paul looked blank.

'Where do you live in Germany?' Ken asked.

'I told you,' Paul replied. 'In the country. Near to Berlin.'

'Married?'

'Not yet,' Paul answered. 'Are you?'

'Not so the Padre would notice it. But there's a girl in Putney who's my wife – all but.'

'All but?'

'All but the ring,' Ken explained.

'Your parents? Do they live?' Paul enquired.

Ken reflected for a moment. 'After a fashion, yes. I suppose you could say they live. My Dad works in a bank, poor bastard. I wouldn't be a clerk in a bank for anything. And my Mum works half the day in the kitchen and the other half in the back yard. And that's about all the pair of them do. Work, work, work, without cease – and worry about me. They deserve better things. That's the truth of it. But I doubt they'll ever get them.'

'Before the war,' Paul asked, "what did you do?'

'Well, I didn't do too much – to tell you the honest truth,' Ken confessed, almost ruefully. 'I'd set my heart on becoming a racing-driver. So after I left school, I got a job as an apprentice-mechanic in a local garage. But the man that owned the place and I didn't see eye to eye over working hours. So after six months of argy-bargy I told him to stuff his spanner where the monkeys stuff their nuts, and walked out. Then I hung around home for a few months, doing sweet FA.'

'Sweet FA?' Paul enquired.

'Sweet Fanny Adams, Sweet Fuck All,' Ken explained. 'Sweet nothing. And when I couldn't bear those reproachful glances over the breakfast table an instant more, I took a job driving a grocer's van. A bloody long way from the race track, as you can see. Then your Herr Hitler went too far. So now I drive a rotten tank. What about you?'

'I am very well, thank you,' Paul replied politely.

'No, I mean this hotel business,' Ken explained.

'My father is the manager in a hotel in Riesbach, a small town about sixty miles to the south of Berlin,' Paul informed him. 'It seemed natural that I should take the same profession as my father ... but I decided to do my training in England.'

'Why England of all places?'

'You have different methods there,' Paul pointed out.

'I'll say we have,' Ken agreed. 'Ever had a meal in Tunbridge Wells?'

'I worked in London.'

'How do you go about training?' Ken asked. 'Watch the barman in the cocktail lounge fiddling the till?'

'You work in various departments of a hotel,' Paul answered. 'I was working as a waiter in a restaurant in London. Charlotte Street. I was sad to leave England. I liked it there. I had made some good friends. But in Germany I was called up. The Fatherland needed me and I came back. I was so glad.'

'Glad?'

'Weren't you glad when you were asked to join the Army?' Paul asked. 'Weren't you glad to be away from your slums and poverty? Away from dirt and filth? Away from all the struggles to earn money?'

Ken threw out his arms and gestured around at the barren desert landscape. 'Glad to be in this bloody wilderness?' he exclaimed in exasperation. 'Glad to be the target of shells and Stukas? Glad to have a tank shot away from under me and my mates slaughtered? Glad to have nearly died of thirst? Glad! You must be bleedin' potty.'

'*Bitte?*'

'You must be a lunatic, mate. Insane. Mad.'

'*Vielleicht*. Perhaps I am mad. But when I heard that we were sailing for Benghazi to join the Afrika Korps under General Rommel, I knew that at last I would have the chance to do something worth the while.'

Ken grunted. 'Like shooting me – for instance,' he suggested.

'Like shooting your tank, Ken,' Paul said. He gave a broad grin. 'Like taking you a prisoner.'

'Well, you've taken me prisoner – till sunset, at least – so I hope you're happy.'

The smile slowly receded from Paul's face; he looked very solemn. '*Jawohl*,' he said. 'I am happy.'

'You're never serious?' Ken enquired in a voice filled with disbelief.

Paul nodded. 'I am most serious,' he said. 'I am happy.'

'But why for Christ's sake?' Ken asked. 'What the hell have you got to be happy about out here – miles from the nearest bint and miles from the nearest boozer?'

'I have fought against the enemy. I have proved myself.'

'Proved yourself what?'

'Proved myself a man.'

'Oh, Great Aunt Maud!'

'But I have. Indeed I have.'

'So your blessed Fatherland has to send out vast convoys of ships laden with thousands of tanks and lorries and crammed with soldiers like sardines in a tin, protected by umbrellas of fighters and bombers, all the way to this sodding stretch of desolate sand, and my dear Motherland has to produce an equal amount of troops and ironmongery – just in order to prove Fritz von whatever your name is of Riesbach that he's a man? I've never heard the like before. You've got to be joking. Wouldn't it have saved a lot of bother all round if you'd just taken a look between your legs?'

Ken stopped speaking and stared at Paul. The German stood up, kicking the ammunition box backwards a little as he did so. His face was flushed and his blue eyes stared coldly at the English soldier. He had to make an effort to control the shaking of his hands. It was obvious that he was deeply angry. Abruptly he turned away from Ken and began to walk away.

Ken sprang to his feet. 'Now where are you going?' Ken demanded, his voice half amused and half serious. 'You can't leave me ... I'm your prisoner, remember? I have to be guarded. Erwin Rommel said so ... Come back. Or I'll report you to Erwin.'

At first, Paul took no heed of Ken. Then his pace slackened. He dawdled forward for a few more steps and stopped walking completely. Slowly he turned back to face Ken; his face was twisted and strained.

'You are no longer my prisoner,' he said in a voice filled with controlled rage. 'You can go.'

'Thanks,' Ken replied sardonically.

Paul moved a few paces back towards Ken. 'You can go,' he repeated. His voice was still thick with anger.

'I heard you the first time,' Ken replied.

'*Gut.*'

The two men faced each other across the narrow strip of sand which divided them. Rapidly Paul stepped forward and slapped Ken hard across the face. Ken's head rocked back from the impact. A red impression of Paul's hand appeared across Ken's cheek. For an instant a look of sheer murderousness fleeted across the Englishman's face; he looked as if he were about to spring at the German. With a great effort of will he controlled himself, the sole sign of anger was in the nervous tic of a muscle at the side of his face. For an instant Ken was very still. He rubbed a hand across his inflamed face. He glared at Paul. When he spoke his voice was low and angry.

'Now why did you have to do that?' Ken asked. 'To prove yourself a man again?'

Paul ignored Ken. He walked briskly past him towards the makeshift bivouac and tested the security of the tarpaulin. 'No,' Paul said in a taut voice as he busied himself with testing and tightening the ropes that held the tarpaulin in place. 'No. I did that so as to teach you not to laugh at me.'

Ken rubbed his hand across his face again. 'Well, you mustn't do it,' he said. 'I might hit back ... and I'm stronger than you are. Or at least I think I am – and that's what matters, or so they tell me.'

'Then don't laugh at me,' Paul insisted.

'I won't talk at all – if that's what you'd prefer,' Ken replied.

'No. You may talk.'

'But not laugh?'

'Not laugh *at me*.'

'Oh, stuff it ...'

Ken began to move idly in the direction of the tank. As he moved around the great iron hulk, he kicked and prodded and pried, lifting hatches and examining. At one instant he lifted a lid on the side of the tank, peered inside, reached inside and carefully pulled out tea and sugar.

'What are you doing?' Paul called.

'Searching ...'

Ken threw a shirt and some socks at Paul, who clumsily caught them and stood holding them in his arms. After watching Ken for a few moments more, Paul turned and walked to the bivouac. He lifted the flap and threw the items of clothing inside. Noticing the empty bully beef tins lying on the sand, Paul stooped and picked them up. Carrying the shovel, clutching the empty tins, Paul walked away from the tank and into the desert.

Ken stopped his search of the tank and stared after the German soldier. 'What on earth are you doing?' Ken called out, observing Paul digging in the sand.

'Burying these tins,' Paul shouted back. 'This place is now my home – however temporary – and I don't want it swarming with flies ...'

Paul dropped the tins into the shallow hole he had dug and piled the sand back on top of them. When the tins were completely covered, he patted it neatly flat and, dragging the shovel behind him, returned to the tank.

'You will find a lot of equipment ...' Paul said, as he leaned against the tank.

Ken ignored him.

Paul's voice now became conciliatory. 'There is even a spare bedroll of blankets,' he announced.

Ken continued to forage around the tank. 'I'll stay the night here,' he declared, 'Kraut or no Kraut.'

'And then?' Paul asked.

Ken did not reply.

'What about tomorrow?' Paul enquired with a slight tremor in his voice.

When Ken finally replied, his voice was still cold and hostile. 'I'm stiff from walking,' he said. 'I may decide to lay up here for a day or two.'

'I shall remain here also,' Paul declared.

Ken continued to work his way around the tank. At last he found what he had been searching for. Lashed to the side of the tank was a bedroll of blankets. Carefully Ken began to untie the knots of the ropes which held the blankets in position.

Paul walked back towards the bivouac, picking up the rucksack, plates and water-bottle on the way. He placed them in the shade of the bivouac and then sat down on the canvas chair.

'I shall remain here also,' Paul repeated.

'That's interesting news,' Ken commented sarcastically.

'I'm better off here than getting lost in the desert again,' Paul explained. 'Besides, we are bound to advance soon and they will find me.'

Ken walked across to the bivouac with the tea and sugar and placed them with the rucksack. He then walked back to the tank and unfastened the cords holding the bedroll. He dragged it out onto the sand at the furthest point from the bivouac and unrolled it.

Suddenly Ken looked across at Paul. 'But *we* might advance,' he said. 'We do sometimes, you know.'

'I will risk it,' Paul stated.

'Please yourself,' Ken told him.

'If I please myself, at least I please someone,' Paul retorted.

'You have a point there, old son,' Ken conceded. 'You might have noticed, I've found some tea and sugar. So I shall please myself by having a cup of char with my supper.'

'But you've only just had lunch,' Paul said in protest.

Ken stared coldly at Paul. 'You might not have noticed it,' he said, 'but the sun is beginning to set. It's a lot cooler now than it was earlier – and a cup of char will warm me up very nicely, thank you.'

The German raised his head and looked around him. Just as Ken had said, the sun was sinking slowly on the horizon, the light was beginning to recede, and the desert evening was cooling down. By nightfall it would be cold enough to require sweaters and a fire.

'You are right, Ken,' Paul said. He paused for a moment and watched as Ken prepared his bedroll. 'My father ... he eats very much,' he announced unexpectedly.

Ken remained busily silent.

'I said my father eats very much,' Paul repeated. 'He is very greedy.'

'Really,' Ken said in a voice heavy with assumed boredom.

'He was always set thick about the shoulders,' Paul continued. 'But around the waist he was slim. Now he is fat like an ox.'

'Is he now?' Ken said with polite sarcasm, reappearing from behind the tank. He walked along the front of the tank, stooping to peer underneath it. He straightened himself and moved along the side of it. He spotted a stick, bent to pick it up and then moved back along the tank, lifted up the left flap and propped it into position with the stick. He was preparing a bivouac for himself.

'My father is quite an important member of the Party in Riesbach,' Paul declared.

'How interesting.'

'He has even met the Führer.'

'Bully for him.'

'He was one of the reception committee – when the Führer came to open the new *Bahnof* in Riesbach – the new station.'

'Was he now?'

'It was in the *Riesbacher Zeitung*. My mother sent me a clipping.'

Ken pulled a second tarpaulin and began to place it in position over the simple structure he had erected.

'I can show you the clipping,' Paul said.

'Don't bother,' Ken muttered. 'I'm not interested.'

Paul dragged his wallet from his pocket, opened it and began to search through it. 'Here it is,' he said proudly, holding out the newspaper clipping to Ken.

Ken stopped his work on his bivouac, tested the ropes holding the tarpaulin in position and nodded to himself. 'That should hold it,' he said. He walked over to Paul and took the newspaper clipping from his outstretched hand.

'Is this your father?' he asked. 'The one with the great pot-belly.'

'*Ja*. That is him.'

'Well I never,' Ken said, passing the cutting back.

Paul replaced the cutting in his wallet and then returned it to his pocket. He extracted the packet of cigarettes and held them out to Ken. 'Cigarette?' he asked.

For a moment Ken hesitated, then he pulled a cigarette from the packet and placed it between his lips. Paul produced his lighter, ignited it and held the flame to the tip of Ken's cigarette.

'Thanks,' Ken said.

There was a brief silence as the two men smoked their cigarettes.

'I'm sorry I hit you,' Paul said in a muffled voice.

'You'll be sorrier still if you try it again,' Ken replied.

As they smoked their cigarettes, the silence became more companionable, the tension slowly relaxed. Once again Paul rummaged in his pocket for his wallet – this time extracting a crumpled postcard and passing it to Ken.

'That was the girl I had in Naples before we embarked ...' Paul told him. 'That's me with her.'

Ken examined the photograph with interest. He licked his lips appreciatively. 'Girl?' he exclaimed. 'She's thirty-five if she's a day ... but not bad with it. And what are you trying to do to the poor tart? Eat her?'

'I went back to her room that very night,' Paul boasted.

'From the appearance of things, I'd say you needed to go back to her room that very instant,' Ken said.

'Have you a photo of your girl?' Paul asked.

'I lost all my clobber when the tank brewed up,' Ken replied.

'I'm sorry,' Paul said.

'Fortunes of war, me old mate,' Ken answered philosophically as he passed the photograph back to Paul. 'I was bloody lucky to get out with my skin intact.'

Paul nodded. 'It gets cold as soon as the sun begins to go down,' he said. 'I will get the primus stove from the bivvy.'

'Primus stove? Does it work?' Ken asked.

Paul nodded. '*Jawohl*. Of course,' he answered.

'We lack for nothing,' Ken said with a grin.

Paul crawled into the bivouac and reappeared a few moments later with a primus stove. Under one arm he had two khaki-coloured sweaters. 'Here,' he said, throwing a sweater to Ken, 'you'd better put this on.'

'Thanks,' Ken acknowledged, as he slipped the sweater over his head.

Paul pulled his own sweater over his head, then began to fiddle with the primus stove.

'I can't believe this,' Ken said.

'There are also two oil-lamps,' Paul told him. 'We have food, water, tea, sugar – I've got everything ready for us.'

Ken laughed. 'You sound as if you were expecting company,' he said.

For an instant Paul was thrown off-guard and he looked worried. 'Actually since I came here three days ago, I have had a feeling that someone might appear from across the desert,' he confessed.

'But not a bloody *Engländer*, I bet,' Ken said.

Paul moved away from the stove and picked up a jerry-can of water. 'No,' he said softly, 'Not an *Engländer* ...'

'An Iti perhaps?'

'No,' Paul answered. 'Not an Iti.'

As they spoke the light was fading from the sky.

'Don't you like Itis, then?' Ken asked, taking the tea and sugar and moving towards the canvas chair. As Ken settled into the chair, Paul returned with the jerry-can.

'Not so much, no,' Paul said.

'Why?'

'Because they are conceited and often they smell of garlic.'

'Don't *Engländers* smell?' Ken enquired.

Paul filled a billy-can with water. He placed it carefully on the stove. He turned and dragged the upturned ammunition box towards him and sat down upon it. 'Oh, yes,' he said, 'but I don't mind it. I don't know why. You smell. But I don't mind it.'

'Memo,' Ken announced. 'Wash pits and parts if we can spare the water. How much water is there?'

'Seven cans,' Paul replied, 'apart from the water in the tank itself.'

'Then I'll wash before turning in,' Ken promised himself.

'Really, I cannot understand your English,' Paul stated. '*Wirklich.*'

After a moment's pause, using his lighter Paul managed to get the primus stove alight.

'You don't hate us really,' he announced, 'and yet you must fight against us. But you should be fighting on our side. You should join us – so that we could fight side by side as friends against the nations who threaten us. You should be fighting with us against the Russians.'

'If I were given the choice, I don't think I'd want to fight anyone,' Ken said.

Paul shook his head. 'Then why do you fight against us?' he asked. 'Because you are hypocrites. You pretend to be shocked when we invade a country. Yet when England was strong she invaded lands all over the world. You raise your hands in horror when we have to kill a few to save many. Yet when England is strong and her air power allows it she slaughters women and children.'

Ken looked startled. 'What's that?' he asked.

'You must know what happened in the raid over Hanover?' Paul insisted.

Ken shook his head. 'No,' he said. 'Tell me.'

'The raid was a mass murder of innocent people,' Paul declared. 'For instance, what had my grandmother done to harm you? She was an invalid who couldn't even move. There were hundreds like her killed. And she always used to say she liked the English. *Das ist sehr komisch, nicht wahr?* She liked you, and you killed her.'

Ken looked solemn; though the faint beginnings of a smile played around the lines of his mouth. 'If my grandmother had her way,' he said slowly, 'every Kraut would be collected from all over the world and put onto a great big island in the middle of the Atlantic. And when she'd got the very last Kraut there, *my* grannie would blow the whole place up and watch it sink. She loathes the lot of you, my grannie does. But that's not going to make it any different for her if a stray bomb finds its way to number seventeen Camelot Grove, Wimbledon. I'm sorry about your grandmother. But when I hear there's been a raid on London I'm apprehensive about mine.'

'But ...'

'Look, why don't we just give grannies a miss for this evening and watch the sunset?'

Ken stood up and stretched. He walked casually towards the tank and rested his back against it. For a while he gazed at Paul.

'If only I could speak English really well, there are so many things I could say,' Paul said.

Ken shifted until he was standing in a more comfortable position. He folded his arms across his chest. 'Such as?' he asked.

'You find life *komisch*. You find it comical,' Paul said, shaking his head. 'I don't understand.'

'Oh, yes ...' Ken said.

He picked up the shovel and drew it in a straight line through the sand; then he pulled the shovel through the sand again – making a line which ran parallel to the first. He moved the shovel through the sand more times, marking lines which intersected with the first pair. On the sand in front of him, Ken had drawn a primitive game of noughts and crosses. He marked an X in the sand. 'Comical?' he said. 'Oh, yes ...'

'Because in life you have always been safe,' Paul stated with determination. 'Never have you been hurt.'

'I wouldn't quite agree with that,' Ken said quietly.

'*Es ist doch wahr, Mensch*,' Paul said. 'I can see it in your face. At home you were loved by your parents. You were always safe. You were never tempted ... in any way. I can see it for certain.'

'All right, then,' Ken conceded. 'But what problems did you have?'

'I left home when I was very young,' Paul said softly, nodding his head and clasping the thumb of his left hand with the palm of his right. 'I left my country,' he continued, and clasped the index finger of his left hand. It was as if he were counting up on the fingers of his hand all of his life's hardships. 'Yes, I had my problems,' he concluded.

'They don't sound so drastic to me,' Ken said, not unkindly. 'And what about studying the hotel business? When you could always go back to Daddy? It all sounds pretty cushy to me, mate.'

'I had problems enough,' Paul insisted.

'Few don't,' Ken said and drew another cross in the pattern in the sand in front of him.

'*Vielleicht.*'

Ken waved the spade in the air. 'Don't tell me you've been using this each morning – all by yourself?'

'*Warum nicht?*'

'Trust a Jerry to obey army orders when his nearest officer's probably a hundred miles a way,' Ken said, glancing towards Paul to gauge his reaction to this remark.

Paul grinned with amusement. 'I told you,' he said, 'if you don't dig deep, you get flies. I thought everyone – except beginners – knew that.'

'How long do you expect to be here, for God's sake? A month?'

Paul shrugged his shoulders. 'How can I tell,' he said.

'Well, I'm not staying here for more than a day or two,' Ken announced firmly. He drew a third cross in the pattern, pulled the spade through the row of crosses in a line, and let it drop to the ground. 'Not much fun playing noughts and crosses on your own,' he muttered, kicking sand over the game. 'I make no secret of the fact; I'm not staying here for longer than necessary.'

'That is for you to decide,' Paul said primly.

'Dead right, old cock,' Ken said strolling towards Paul's bivouac. He lifted the tarpaulin flap. 'Now what have we here,' he said, pulling a mouth-organ from the pocket of a jacket which was hanging just inside the opening. Ken held the mouth-organ aloft. 'Look what I've found,' he exclaimed.

Paul darted towards Ken. 'Give it back,' he called. 'That's mine.'

Ken dodged away from Paul and began to hurry away into the desert. Paul hastened after him across the soft sand.

'That's mine!' Paul called out, panting for breath as he stumbled in the sand.

Ken did not stop running, though he was careful to make sure he was always in view of the tank. 'Bet you pinched it off the tank,' Ken called out, puffing.

'No, it's mine,' Paul cried out in sudden desperation. 'Look at the make. It's made in Germany. It's mine, I tell you.'

Ken stopped running. He turned round and stared back at Paul who was no more than a few yards away from him. 'All right,' Ken said, still out of breath. 'Don't get excited.'

He lifted the mouth-organ to his lips.

'Stop!' Paul ordered.

'*Now* what is it?' Ken asked in a voice tinged with exasperation.

'No one must play it except myself,' Paul said. 'It's mine. I've had it for five years.'

Ken began to move back towards the tank, dodging away from Paul who trailed dejectedly along behind him. Once back within the perimeter of their makeshift camp, Ken made a dash for the canvas chair and collapsed into it. He held the mouth-organ in front of him and made a great display of carefully examining it.

'Made in Germany,' Ken read, 'All right, I believe you.'

Ken tossed the mouth-organ towards Paul, who caught it neatly in his right hand. He held the musical instrument in a way which seemed almost protective.

Ken gazed towards the horizon. 'You're supposed to see a green flash when the sun goes down,' he said. 'But you never do. Another of life's little disappointments. Come to the desert they say, see the green flash. You come – and what do you get? Flies up your nostrils, sand up your arsehole and your head shot off. Someday somebody's going to complain.'

Absolutely without motion, Ken sat watching the fading light. Paul stood by his side, gazing at the vanishing rays of the sun. Suddenly he shivered.

'Cold?' Ken asked.

Paul shook his head. 'No. I was just thinking. When you're down there inside the tank … they begin to get your range …'

Ken spoke quietly, picking up the sentence Paul had been

about to speak. The moment of a common shared memory seemed to draw them closer.

'The fittings begin crashing back on you ...' Ken said.

Paul shuddered. 'You know that if you're hit ...'

'You're trapped ...'

'In the turret,' Paul said, 'you're pressed so tight you can hardly move. The crack of the gun is so loud – when it fires it seems to break your ears.'

'Give me the pier at Brighton – without the rifle-range.'

'Do you think ...' Paul began, breaking off abruptly.

'Do I think what?' Ken asked.

'If they get you – if you're killed, do you think there's anything?'

For a moment Ken was lost in thought. 'To tell you the truth – I've never been sure,' he said. 'But when you see the dead lying around in this desert – they certainly do look very dead. But we're alive – not that we mean very much to anyone or anything. But what *does* matter? That's what I'm always wondering. But what's the point of thinking about it?'

Ken stood up and picked up a dixie-pot and the jerry-can. He walked away from the bivouac, towards the tank. He placed the dixie on the side of the tank and poured water from the can into it.

'We've been lucky,' Paul muttered.

Ken began to peel off his sweater. 'That's one way of considering it,' he said. He continued to strip off his clothes until he was naked. He began to splash water on his body.

'God, that feels good,' he said.

Paul glanced towards Ken, then looked away.

Ken picked up the sweater and, using it as a towel, started to rub himself dry. He looked across at Paul.

'Well, go on,' Ken said, indicating the mouth-organ, 'play the thing.'

Paul smiled and lifted the mouth-organ to his lips. He shook it to remove any sand which might have become trapped inside. He smiled at Ken and then began to play 'Lili Marlene'. As Paul played, Ken took up the tune and began to whistle along with it. Then he broke off.

'That's nice,' he said. 'Funny how that song's caught on with both sides.'

Paul stopped playing and lowered the mouth-organ from his mouth. He clasped it gently in his hand. 'Not really so,' he said. 'Because it's a soldier's song. It was written by a German soldier in the last war.'

'It's still odd how it's caught on.'

'With us, I know why,' Paul said. 'At least, I think I do ...'

'Why then?'

'Because ... because ... it tells us that it's probably hopeless. But we must go on – because we can never stop. We must go on longing for ever.'

'Longing for what? For God's sake.'

Paul turned away from Ken and stared out at the darkness which had closed like a shroud around them. At this moment the desert seemed flat and smooth – like an endless and bottomless black lake. It was very dark, it was very still – and it was very empty. Yet the sheer vastness and emptiness had a curiously humbling effect. When he spoke, Paul almost whispered.

'I don't know quite ...' he said. 'It is more like ... just ... longing.'

'What have you got to long for?' Ken asked quietly.

Paul gave a rueful smile. 'Perhaps I'll tell you one day,' he said and raised the mouth-organ once more to his lips and continued to play the plaintive tune of 'Lili Marlene'.

3

During most of the following day, Ken and Paul spent much of the time in their respective bivouacs which at least afforded some kind of shade from the hideous, unrelenting glare of the fierce desert sun. At intervals one or other of them would crawl out into the heat to make a brew of tea or to get a tin of bully beef and some biscuits. The oppressive heat subdued any desire for further activity.

Neither man had any thoughts about moving from the area of the camp. A strange sense of security pervaded the being of both men. Both had suffered the nightmare of being lost in the wilderness. Though neither would admit it to himself, they had no desire to venture out into the bleak world of endlessly rolling sand so soon after their ordeals.

In the cramped, makeshift shelter of his bivouac, Ken had time to take stock. As he lay curled up in the blankets of his bedroll, he knew that he would have to attempt to regain the British lines. But how was he to do this without a compass? He could try navigating by the stars – though he didn't set much store by this. Ken was London born and bred, he was aware that what little he knew about the relative positions of the stars could be written on the back of a postage stamp. He wasn't at all sure that he could even identify the Pole Star. Ruefully Ken reflected that the only times he had paid any attention to the sky at night had been when lying flat on his back in the grass, relaxing after his exertions with one of the many girls from Fulham, Hammersmith or Putney whom he had dated.

Ken could easily imagine himself setting out into the

vastness of the desert – alone, without a compass, with little hope of being able to find direction from a sky full of stars which had no purposeful meaning for him. It would be a disaster. He would probably end up wandering around in ever-increasing circles, hopelessly lost. Ken could envisage himself staggering along in the cool desert night, lurching with fatigue, yet dragging himself onward, placing one foot before the other in an endless pattern of repetition until finally he dropped from sheer exhaustion. He didn't fancy that. He didn't fancy lying on the burning sand in the merciless heat of the day – and he knew that he would not be able to travel when the sun was high in the sky – with his body fluids evaporating until he was totally dehydrated, dead, a corpse as mummified as that as any of those Egyptian Pharaohs he could remember seeing on a school outing to the British Museum.

Dying in the desert while fighting in a tank was one thing – it was something which every man thought about, a secret fear with which each man learned to live. But to die in a blazing tank was almost heroic – and it certainly wasn't the horrifying solitary death he could face if he set off alone into the desert. To Ken, there was something obscene about the thought of dying alone in this alien place – of having his bleached bones picked over by the scavenging birds and small rats and scuttling reptiles.

As he dozed in his bedroll, Ken felt the tautness and strain easing from his tired muscles. His flesh wound was no longer painful and he knew it would quickly heal. Food and drink had replenished his weary body, sleep had helped restore the equanimity of his tired mind. This lonely camp into which he had gratefully stumbled seemed like a haven of peace and comfort after the rigours of his experiences in the desert. There was food and water for several days at least. It was a safe billet – and Ken knew he would stay until he had formed a plan.

Paul was far more restless than Ken. He hadn't had the length of time lost in the desert that the English soldier had experienced. Yet as he pottered around the camp during the course of the day – for it was generally he who prepared the tea and opened tins of meat for the English soldier – his mind was troubled. As he dug the deep latrine holes among the camel-grass away from the back of the tank, Paul found himself wondering about Ken, wishing to know more about this strange *komisch* character.

In the burning heat of high noon, as the sun glared down so fiercely it seemed to bleach all colour from the sky, Paul lay on top of his sleeping bag – naked but for his shorts. He could feel the rivulets of sweat trickling down his chest, matting the blond hair of his armpits. He was aware of the not unpleasant odour of his body as he moved restlessly. It was too hot to sleep, it was too hot to take any form of exercise. It was too hot to do anything except remain as still as possible and look forward to the late afternoon when the fierceness of the sun would at least be somewhat abated.

Idly, Paul flipped through the pages of a paperback novel. It did not greatly interest him, and he found it impossible to concentrate on the words on the page in front of him. The desert heat seemed to be melting his brain – or frying it. The words on the page seemed to run together until they formed a damp black blur. Restlessly he heaved himself upright into a sitting position. He dropped the book onto the sand. Wearily he ran a hand through his white-blond hair. He stared across the burning sand at the still figure of Ken in his bivouac. For a moment Paul sat completely immobile, looking across at the other bivouac. Then he relaxed his pose and fell back onto the sleeping bag.

Slowly the sun made its progress across the sky and as the day drifted towards evening and the sun moved nearer to the horizon life became bearable again.

Ken, feeling considerably refreshed, made another search of the tank. He was pleased to find a razor, some blades and shaving soap. Almost contentedly he lathered his face and cautiously dragged the razor across the thick black stubble on his face. Finishing his shave, Ken splashed water on his face to wash away the remaining suds. The long rest, the food he had eaten and the drink he had consumed, most of all the shave, now made Ken look far younger.

At sunset, Paul and Ken pulled on their khaki sweaters against the chill of the evening which contrasted so sharply with the heat of the day. They began to bustle about preparing their simple supper, thick slices of bully beef atop two army biscuits each. With their meal, they drank a strong brew of tea.

'Army biscuits,' Ken said through a mouthful of crumbs, 'for the first time they taste good. And the advantage of having them in tins is that they never go stale.'

'In the rations in our tank,' Paul commented, 'in our rations there are bars of chocolate especially made full of vitamins.'

'Well, you haven't got a tank now, so stop talking about it,' Ken said good humouredly.

Paul smiled at him. 'But I have got a tank,' he said. 'This one here is my tank. I captured it.'

'Now don't start *that* all over again,' Ken said. Then he smiled at Paul. 'But I suppose you can call it your tank if you really want to.'

'*Bestimmt*,' Paul answered. 'I certainly will.'

They finished eating and sat quietly sipping their tin mugs of tea. The night was very still and the surrounding desert seemed to shine in the white light of the full moon. An oil-lamp shed a comforting circle of light from its position on an upturned ammunition box. The second lamp glowed softly by the front of Paul's bivouac.

Paul stood up and moved over to his bivouac. He settled himself comfortably on his sleeping-bag and picked up the paperbacked novel with which he had been struggling earlier in the day. As his eyes travelled down the page, a smile spread across his face. Paul gave a low whistle as he flicked the page.

Ken, again seated in the canvas chair, stared up at the moon. For a while he seemed lost in thought. He directed his gaze towards Paul.

'Know anything about astrology?' Ken asked.

'*Gar nichts*,' Paul replied without taking his eyes from his book. 'Sweet nothing – as you would say.'

Ken took some binoculars, hanging from the back of the chair which he had found earlier on the tank. He peered through them and then lifted them up towards the sheltering sky.

'Well,' he said, 'if you were on the star I've been staring up at, and you looked back, you'd see the Gippos building the pyramids – and you'd see King Pharaoh and Queen Nefertiti a-necking in the bullrushes.'

Paul looked up from his book. 'Pharaoh and Nefertiti weren't in the bullrushes,' he said. 'That was Moses.'

'Well, someone must have been a-doing it in the bullrushes for Moses to have got there in the first place,' Ken commented drily.

'In a science magazine I once read, it says that before the end of the century men will have reached the moon.'

'Poor moon,' Ken said, focussing the binoculars on Paul. 'What's that large book you're reading?'

'I found it on the tank,' Paul replied. 'It's called *The Crimson Moll*.'

'The Crimson what?' Ken asked.

'*The Crimson Moll*,' Paul answered. 'MOLL. What *is* a moll?'

Ken lowered the binoculars and let them rest in his lap. He chuckled and snatched the book from Paul's grasp.

'You've been reading this book all day,' he said, holding the battered volume up. 'Surely you've found out by now?'

'Is it part of a woman's body?' Paul asked.

'Leave it out,' Ken said. 'Don't be so daft. It's American for a tart ... A kept woman, a painted lady of easy virtue. A whore of Babylon with great big tits.'

Ken dropped the book in the sand in front of Paul.

'You speak so well,' Paul said smiling up at him. 'I wonder you're not an officer.'

'I've wondered for quite a long time myself,' Ken replied. 'But the Selection Board didn't even bother to wonder. They took one look at Preston, Kenneth George – and they gave their verdict. "Preston," they said, "we've examined your qualifications most carefully. We note that you have

proved a proficient tank driver and an exemplary soldier."
They use long words like that because it covers up their
ignorance. "We also note," they continued, "that you weren't
at a public school, you haven't a private income, and you
don't play polo – which disqualified you from entering any
regiment of Lancers or Hussars. We further observe from your
record that you've had your collar felt – which puts the final
Kybosh on your getting commissioned in the Tank Corps. So
you'll stay in the tanks, Trooper Preston, and you'd better
learn to like it – because that's your lot." '

'What does it mean to have your collar felt?' Paul asked.

'Oh, that's just an expression.'

'But what does it mean?'

'Oh, it means to have been – to have been at a state school.
What's that book of yours like?'

'Very hot stuff,' Paul said smirking.

'Then give,' Ken said. 'Read us some.'

Paul picked up the book and turned the pages until he
found a passage which attracted his attention. ' "Unwillingly
she unfastened her blouse",' he read, ' "while his dark eyes
were fixed on her gloatingly." '

'On her what?'

'Gloatingly,' Paul repeated. " 'With a sigh, close to despair,
she removed her brassiere. Her breasts were like small water-
melons ..." '

'Very tasty.'

' "Her skin was taut and smooth. She glared at him
defiantly. At that moment he produced his weapon".'

Ken jerked up in his seat. 'His what?'

Paul grinned. ' "At that moment he produced his
weapon",' he read again.

'I don't believe you!' Ken exclaimed grabbing the book
away from Paul. He stared at the page, his lips moving silently
for a moment. He glanced towards Paul and laughed. ' "At
that moment he produced his weapon",' he read, ' "a small
luger ..." '

Paul burst out into uproarious laughter.

Ken slapped him gently on the head with the book. 'You

crafty bleedin' Kraut,' he said, laughing himself. 'Trying to mislead an innocent *Engländer*.'

Paul heaved himself to his feet. 'I had you fooled, *ja*?' He said trying to suppress his laughter.

Ken stuck out a leg and as Paul moved, he tripped over it.

'You treacherous Kraut bastard,' Ken said.

'You dirty *Engländer*!'

As he clambered onto his feet again, Paul scooped up a handful of sand and threw it towards Ken.

'I'm not dirty,' Ken announced. 'I washed myself all over only last night. I left not one part of me untouched – as you certainly witnessed.'

'Dirty in the mind,' Paul amended.

'Ah well, now that's a different matter,' Ken agreed.

Paul sat down again and picked up the book.

'Read us some more ...' Ken suggested.

' "Take off all your clothes",' Paul read. ' "I want you wholly naked." '

'The wicked old man,' Ken exclaimed.

' "With trembling fingers she unzipped her skirt",' Paul read. ' "Her thighs gleamed white as ivory. Then she removed ..." '

'Stop!' Ken cried. 'Enough! I can't stand it! You're getting me all worked up ...'

Ken got to his feet and started to pace back and forth on the sand. Suddenly he banged the flat of his hand down hard on the tank.

'And I haven't had a bint for over three months. Fuck ... Fuck the Western Desert. Fuck Rommel. Fuck the Krauts – bar yourself, of course. Fuck the Eighth Army, fuck the whole bleedin' war ... I'm heading back for our lines. Then I shall go sick ... Probably by then I'll be sick anyhow ... Mental fatigue and sexual starvation. "What ails you, Preston, my man?" the MO will ask me.'

Ken's voice suddenly became hoarse. ' "I think, sir, I must have got laryngitis ...",' he said. ' "Open your mouth, my man. Say 'Ah' ..." the MO will ask. "Aaaah!" He will reel back in shock. "Not so loud, my man. And not so strong. You don't know the strength of your own breath." "No, sir, I don't. That's the truth of it. Since my concussion I don't know nothing." "Concussion? ... Oh well, never mind ... A few months sick-leave in Alex will soon put you to rights." "Can't I stay with my regiment, sir? It would just break my heart to leave my comrades." I'm really quite a good actor. "Corporal Doakes ..." the officer will say. "Sah." "Corporal Doakes, this man is seriously ill. Quite deranged in fact. Put him down for three months sick-leave, and see he gets a place on the next convoy back to the Delta ..." "Sah! ..." "Thank you, Corporal." "Sah!" "Arbuthnot ..." "The name's Preston, sir ..." "Very good, Preston. Try not to fret too much ..." "Right, sir, I'll do my best. Goodbye, sir ..." "Goodbye, Pemberton ... Next man!" ' '

Paul gazed up at Ken in wide-eyed amazement. '*Fabelhaft!*' he exclaimed.

'I shall leave this enchanting spot tomorrow,' Ken declared.

'You said that this morning,' Paul said. 'But I know you don't mean it – *Gott sei Dank.*'

'I shall bid you adieu,' Ken declared. 'And I shall piss off east to rejoin our lines. Compass or no compass.'

'But I wouldn't be too sure of reaching the Delta,' Paul said.

'Why not?' Ken asked.

Paul smiled benignly at him. 'Because Erwin might get there first.'

Ken kicked some sand at Paul and then sat down on the sand next to him.

'Why wasn't Rommel born English,' Ken sighed.

'Don't you have *any* Generals?'

'Oh yes, scores of them,' Ken said in a voice full of doom and despair. 'They swarm about GHQ in Cairo like wasps round a jam-jar, or flies round shit. They draw lots to see which one is going to be allowed to wage the next big battle. The winning General goes whizzing up the desert road to Alex, changes all the last one's orders, has all the tanks and lorries painted a different colour – or decides to disguise all the tanks as lorries and all the lorries as tanks – just so as to confuse the enemy and his own side. Then, when he's got everyone so mixed up they don't know their head from their arsehole, the new General launches his attack ... He advances two hundred miles and gets a knighthood. Then he withdraws three hundred miles and gets the sack ... Then they all meet at GHQ to draw lots again. And another bloody General looms up the desert road to take command ... It's a fucking farce. You can have the Delta. But just give us Rommel.'

Paul held out a packet of cigarettes. 'Cigarette?' he asked.

'Ta,' Ken said, extracting a cigarette.

'Do you know,' Ken said, 'we captured a German staff car the other day with Rommel's "appreciation" of the Allied forces in the desert. "The British Tommy fights with courage and tenacity." That's what Rommel says. "The British junior officer shows fine initiative. But the British High Command is unwieldy and cumbersome." He might also have added, "and totally brainless". Because whoever thought up last week's "patrol in force" ought to have his knackers nicked.'

'The Italians have bad Generals too,' Paul said as if to console him.

'Yes. But they've got mobile brothels to make up for it,' Ken declared.

'I never know when you're serious and when you're not serious,' Paul complained.

'Mobile brothels are a very serious business, old cock,' Ken said with a grin. 'Still, on a more serious note – am I the prisoner today – or is it your turn?'

'You are my prisoner,' Paul announced firmly.

'I only ask because these lamps must shine for miles around in the desert,' Ken explained. 'It would look a bit odd if a convoy turned up and there we were, sitting side by side, smoking fags, not knowing which one was the prisoner.'

'It will also look odd if they find that I have the revolver, and you have the bullets,' Paul pointed out.

'Yes,' Ken nodded. 'By the way, where is the revolver?'

'Here,' Paul said lifting the corner of the sleeping bag. He handed the revolver to Ken.

'Ta.' Ken took the bullets from his pocket, broke open the chamber of the gun, and slipped each bullet into place. He closed the gun with a click. With a gesture of exaggerated politeness, Ken handed the gun back to Paul.

'*Danke*,' Paul said and put the revolver into the large Dixie-pot in which they usually boiled water.

Ken stood up. He tugged the binoculars from the back of the chair and walked over to the tank. After climbing onto the main structure of the tank, Ken raised the binoculars to his eyes and stared out at the desert. He ranged the binoculars left and right but there was nothing in any direction. He lowered the lenses and looked up at the moon. After a moment of silent contemplation of the great silver orb, Ken turned his gaze out towards the gleaming barren sands of the desert.

Paul moved over to the tank and looked up at Ken. 'Do you see anything?' he asked.

'Yes,' Ken said.

'What?' Paul asked excitedly.

Ken's voice was flat and emotionless when he spoke. 'Sand,' he said. 'Sand, sand and more fucking sand.'

He jumped from the tank and landed beside Paul.

Paul punched lightly at Ken's chest.

Ken laughed. 'Gotcha that time, didn't I?' he said grinning.

Paul looked solemn. 'I begin to wonder if a convoy will ever find us,' he said.

'Days might go by,' Ken said. 'We'll be all right for water – look at the rain we caught in the tarpaulin last night. But when we run out of food, there'll be nothing for it – I shall have to eat you. I wonder what roast Kraut tastes like.'

'Better than fried *Engländer*,' Paul answered. '*Sagen Sie mir etwas.*'

'Eh?'

'Tell me something, Ken.'

'Anything you like.'

'Why did you have your collar felt!' Paul asked.

'So you *do* know what it means?'

'*Nein*. I guessed,' Paul replied. 'But why were you in prison?'

'Who says I was in prison?'

'But you were,' Paul insisted, 'weren't you?'

'Skip it.'

'I want to know.'

'Why do you?' Ken demanded.

'Because I try to understand you,' Paul explained.

'It's not very difficult.'

'Why were you sentenced to prison?' Paul insisted.

'Forget it.'

'*Aber warum*? Why, Ken?' Paul asked, gently kicking Ken on the ankle.

'It's not "Vy, Ken?" ' Ken said, imitating Paul's German accent. 'It's "Why, Ken?" '

'Then why, Ken?'

Ken hesitated. He gave a long sigh which seemed to come from some deep and lonely place inside of him. He raised his head and looked directly at Paul.

'I fell in love,' he said. 'I fell in love and I've regretted it ever since.'

'What did you regret?' Paul asked.

'The time in nick for a start,' Ken answered.

'But what did you do?'

'All right, if it gives you any pleasure,' Ken said. 'Place – Wimbledon Common, London. Near where me granny lives. Time – four years ago.'

4

It was a sunny afternoon in early June. The air was pleasantly warm and the sense of summer turned people's thoughts away from the struttings and posturing of Adolf Hitler, the German dictator whose political demands seemed to be becoming more and more outrageous with every utterance. Currently there was a subtle sense of unease settling over the whole country as the German leader plotted and schemed his next move. The newspapers were full of stories about Hitler's intentions towards the tiny country of Czechoslovakia which had only come into being after the First World War. Mr Winston Churchill, whom many people in the Conservative Party regarded as a dangerous renegade, constantly warned against the threat the Nazi leader posed to the civilised world. But, generally, his words went unheeded, or were treated with scorn or derision. Yet war did seem to be looming again on the horizon. Though the threat against peace was apparent, few people wished to acknowledge that the old enemy could again be preparing for battle. Another war was unthinkable after the horrors of the Great War; the War to End All Wars.

As Ken strolled across Putney Bridge, stopping midway to gaze down at the murky waters of the river, he remembered his father's conversation at breakfast that morning.

'It couldn't happen again,' Henry Preston had declared emphatically as he sipped at his breakfast cup of tea. 'Another war would be unthinkable. They're not that mad.'

Ken wasn't so sure about that, but he didn't say anything. He knew how much his father hated to be contradicted. He watched as his father raised the tea cup to his mouth and took a genteel sip from it. Small droplets of the liquid caught on the neat moustache his father affected, giving it a faintly disreputable air which didn't go at all well with the prim bank clerk personality. Weak blue eyes glinted from behind metal rimmed spectacles.

'Mr Chamberlain knows what he's doing,' his father had continued. 'He knows how to handle Herr Hitler. He'll make sure there isn't another war.'

Ken's mother, busy at the cooker preparing fried bread and eggs, turned towards them. 'War, war, war. That's all you hear these days,' she said. 'It's a lovely day. Can't you talk about something a bit cheerful for a change?'

Doris Preston slid eggs and slices of fried bread onto the two plates she had been warming on top of the grill and brought them over to the table. She placed a plate of food in front of her husband and the other in front of Ken. She sat down at the table and, lifting the big brown teapot, refilled the cups. She added milk and spoonsful of sugar.

'Ta, Mum,' Ken said, tucking into his food. 'Just what the doctor ordered. I'm starving.'

'It's a wonder you don't put on weight,' Doris said. 'You certainly eat enough.'

Ken dunked a piece of bread into the yolk of his egg and stuffed it into his mouth. 'That's right, Mum,' he said. 'That's because I'm a growing boy.'

'Don't talk with your mouth full,' Doris reprimanded. She beamed at Ken proudly. 'I don't know where you put it all,' she said.

His father set his knife and fork neatly across his empty plate. 'Not only are you a growing boy,' he said, 'you are also a bone-idle one. When do you intend to get a job?'

Ken wiped a slice of bread around his plate and took a bite from it. He chewed vigorously for a moment and then he swallowed his mouthful of food.

'I keep looking,' he mumbled.

'That's right, Dad,' Doris said. 'Don't go on at the boy. He's trying, you know.'

'He's trying, all right,' Henry said grimly, pushing his plate away from him. Then his expression softened and he smiled at Ken. 'What do you intend to do with yourself today, son?' he asked.

Ken gulped down a mouthful of tea. He wiped his hand across his mouth to dry his lips. 'Don't know,' he said. 'Might mosey out to Wimbledon and see Gran.'

Doris rattled the dirty breakfast plates in the sink. 'That's a good idea,' she said. 'I know she'd love to see you.'

Later in the morning, after he had digested his breakfast and skimmed through the pages of his father's *News Chronicle*, Ken set off for his grandmother's home in Wimbledon. As he hadn't worked for over three months he was very short of money – dependent, in fact, on the few shillings his mother could spare him from her weekly house-keeping allowance. The motorcycle which was his pride and joy was out of action – and there was no way he could afford to pay to have it repaired. He would have to walk. Having no money was a real bore, but at least he didn't have to put up with the petty nagging of his boss at his previous job – there had always been complaints that Ken didn't make his grocery deliveries quickly enough. 'Sod him, for a lark,' Ken thought to himself. Maybe he shouldn't have spent quite so much time in the pub – but what harm did a lunchtime pint with a few mates do anyone? It was just unfortunate that one of the busy-bodies he delivered to had spotted the van parked outside The Cadogan Arms and reported her discovery to Mr Harridge. Still, being fired wasn't such a hardship. He'd manage until something else turned up.

The walk to Wimbledon was really quite pleasant. He wasn't in any hurry and once he had left the mean streets of Fulham behind, he began to enjoy himself. At the middle of Putney Bridge, Ken stopped and stared down at the murky waters of the Thames. Small craft passed back and forth under the bridge – and he could imagine the bigger ocean-going vessels further down-river, loading and unloading their cargoes and preparing for voyages which would take them all around the globe. 'Travel,' Ken reflected. 'It must be great to get away to some far-off place.'

He crossed the bridge and began to walk up the High Street, pausing to look in shop windows. His pace was easy – he had no reason to hurry, but he noticed he was a bit out of breath. At the top of Putney Hill he sat down on a wooden seat and lit up a cigarette. He smoked in contented silence, watching the traffic straggling up the hill and the passers-by going about their business. He finished smoking and dropped the butt on the pavement between his feet. He ambled along the Park Side, the easy down hill route which ran alongside the wide green expanse of Wimbledon Common. The trees which overhung the pavement gave a welcome and cooling shelter from the afternoon sun; all the exertions of his walk were making him sweat and he looked forward to arriving at his destination and having a refreshing cup of tea with his grandmother.

Ken walked briskly along the Worple Road, then he turned right along Camelot Grove. He stopped at number seventeen, pushed open the little wooden gate and went up the short path to the front door. He lifted the gleaming brass knocker and gave a sharp rat-tat-tat. The sound echoed in the hallway of the tiny terraced house. As he stood on the door-step, Ken gazed at the privet hedge. It was badly in need of cutting.

'Once I've had a cuppa,' Ken thought, 'I'll get out the shears and trim it a bit. That'll please the old girl.'

A little Ford chugged down the road, the noise making Ken aware that there was no sign of life from the house. He knocked on the door again. 'She must be out,' he thought. He wasn't sure if he should wait or not. He knew that if his grandmother were visiting one of her friends in the neighbourhood she could be gone for hours – happily nattering away on an endless stream of cups of tea and the click-click of knitting needles. Ken had never been able to understand why both his mother and his grandmothers rarely went anywhere without a bag of wool, needles, pattern and whatever garment they were currently working on.

After a few moments of indecision – and a few regrets for the cup of tea – he trudged back down the path and began the return walk towards Fulham.

As he moved along Park Side he decided that he would take a walk on the Common. The shade of the trees was inviting and the fresh smell of the grass and the warm soil tempted him. He walked aimlessly for a few moments, breathing in the clean fresh air and listening to the sound of birds in the trees. After a while he found a secluded spot and lay down on the grass. An oak tree towered above him and he could peer up at the clear blue sky through the shape of the branches and leaves. Absently, he chewed on a blade of grass.

Ken felt wonderfully relaxed; slowly he could feel himself drifting off into a light sleep. Abruptly, the still of the afternoon was punctured by a gentle trembling of the ground and the pounding sound of the hooves of a cantering horse. Looking up, propping himself on his elbows, Ken observed the shape of a horse and rider coming towards him. The bright sun in his eyes caused the shapes to be rather indistinct at first but as the horse and rider drew closer Ken observed that the horse was very black and that the rider was a young girl with flying blonde hair and a clear fair skin. It was this startling contrast that first interested him; but as the horse and rider galloped past him, Ken realised that the girl was remarkably beautiful. She didn't appear to be very old, probably no more than fifteen or sixteen, but she had about her a suggestion of self-assurance which made her appear older than her apparent years. As the girl disappeared from his sight, Ken realised that he had been so taken by her appearance that his heart was pounding in his breast.

He struggled to his feet and stood panting, waiting for his heart to calm into a more normal rhythm. He cursed himself. Why hadn't he been wide awake and on his feet? Had he been more alert he could have called some greeting to the girl. Instead he had been half-asleep, stretched out on the grass. A vision of the girl remained fixed in his mind. He realised that he wanted to see her again and, if at all possible, to meet her and get to know her.

Shaking his head vaguely, as if he could hardly believe the image which had flashed so briefly before his eyes, Ken trudged across the Common. Slowly he made his way home.

The girl on the horse became an obsession with Ken. Each afternoon he would walk to the Common and pace the stretch of green where he had seen the blonde girl in the hope that she would again ride his way. Day after day Ken haunted the ·Common – and day after day there was no sign of the girl. Ken began to believe that perhaps the girl had been riding only because she was in the neighbourhood, maybe staying with a friend. Possibly the girl came from some district far away from Wimbledon; he might never see her again. Ken became tormented with a longing to see the girl. She had become an ideal – a fantasy to be cherished and, he hoped, to be fulfilled.

At about five o'clock one afternoon, tired and disheartened, Ken decided to give up his walk and rather than trudge all the way back to Fulham on foot take a bus home. After he had made his decision, Ken's spirits lifted a little and he walked briskly off the Common and along the road to the bus stop. There was a short queue which he joined. He stood idly for a while, watching the road for a sign of the bus. The other people in the queue shuffled their feet restlessly. Ken noticed how no one took any notice of any of the others in the waiting line; they were strangers, locked away in their private compartments and it would take something especially unusual to get them to communicate.

Ken wished he had a newspaper or a magazine to read. Inactivity bored him. He found himself staring down at the bunch of artificial cherries perched on top of the black raffia hat of the woman in front of him. Suddenly a smell of perfume drifted towards him. He was aware that someone had joined the queue and was now standing behind him. The perfume had a clean, fresh smell like wild flowers. Ken turned his head slightly to see what the woman behind him was like.

With a start of recognition, Ken recognised the girl he had come to think of as 'his girl'. Though she was just as lovely as he had remembered, Ken realised with dismay that she was far younger than he had thought. The girl couldn't have been more than fourteen. Quickly Ken turned away. The fascination with the girl was too strong, however, and he looked back to gaze at her again. She was very slim, with soft green eyes. Her mouth was wide and her lips had a sensual look about them. The girl was dressed in a box-pleated skirt and a blue angora cardigan over a plain white cotton blouse. Her fair hair fell to her sloping shoulders. There was no doubt about it: the girl was extremely beautiful, a tantalising mixture of innocence and sensuality.

Ken racked his brain for some suitable expression which would enable him to speak to the girl.

He smiled at her. 'If you're in a real hurry,' he said, 'you can take my place in the queue. I'm in no hurry at all.'

The girl smiled back at him. 'Nor am I, come to that,' she said. 'I'm just on an errand for my mother.'

A feeling of happiness suffused Ken: the girl *did* live in this district then.

'Where are you going to?' he asked.

'Putney.'

'I'm going to Putney, too,' Ken said quickly. 'Let's try and get seats together.'

The girl gave a faint smile. 'Okay,' she said. 'I don't mind.'

Ken thought for a moment. 'Where do you live?' he asked.

The girl gave a mischievous little grin. 'Mother has always told me not to talk to strange men – certainly not to give them our address,' she said.

'Very sound advice,' Ken agreed. 'But we're not strangers any more. At least, I hope we're not.'

'I suppose you're right,' the girl said grinning.

Ken noticed that her teeth were small and neat and very white.

'But I don't even know your name,' the girl said.

As she spoke, Ken was conscious of the woman in the black raffia hat standing in the queue in front of him. He knew she was listening intently to the conversation. He turned his head towards her for a moment, noting that the cherries on top of the hat bobbed slightly as the woman looked away from the direction of Ken and the young girl.

Ken gave a mock bow. 'Ken Preston of Oakridge Road, Fulham,' he said. 'At your service. Now. What's *your* name?'

'Penelope,' the girl announced. 'Penelope Heath. But everyone calls me Penny.'

'So now that we're on christian name terms, I'm no longer a stranger to you and you can tell me your address – or at least the name of the street where you live.'

'All right,' Penny said. 'It's Grove End Road, just off Ridgeway.'

Ken laughed. 'Very posh,' he said. 'And now I can track you down.'

'I don't like the sound of the word "track",' Penny said, a slight expression of alarm fleeting across her face. 'You don't think I'm making it up, do you? Because I can promise you I haven't.'

Ken shook his head. 'I believe you,' he said. 'But thousands wouldn't.'

The bus arrived and several people stepped off. Ken followed Penny onto the bus and climbed the stairs to the top deck. There were plenty of empty seats, and the two of them sat down together halfway along the bus.

'What stop do you want?' Ken asked, taking some coins from his pocket.

'Putney Station,' Penny said.

Ken paid the conductor, who punched two tickets and handed them to Ken.

'Penny,' Ken began, 'there's a question I want to ask you.'

'You're full of questions, aren't you?' Penny said.

'Maybe I'm naturally inquisitive,' Ken answered flippantly.

He felt wildly exultant. He couldn't believe that not only had he found Penny but that he was sitting next to her on the top of a bus having a friendly conversation.

'What's your question, then?' Penny inquired.

'How old are you, Penny?'

Penny was silent for a moment. 'How old do you *think* I am?' she asked.

'I'm not very good at guessing games,' Ken admitted. 'But I'd say you were fourteen.'

'I'm nearly fifteen,' Penny said. 'Don't look so shocked. You must have met girls of my age before, plenty of them are at work by now. Anyhow, I look older.'

'Perhaps,' Ken said slowly. 'But there's a law, isn't there?'

'So *that's* what you were after when you turned around and stared at me like that,' Penny said. She nudged Ken in the ribs. 'You're a dirty old man.'

Ken blushed. 'Not necessarily,' he mumbled.

Penny looked intently at him. 'And what exactly does that mean?' she asked.

Ken was silent for a while. His mind was in a turmoil. Penny might be only fourteen, yet she showed an astonishing ease with him and a surprising awareness that suggested she might have a knowledge beyond her years. His body tingled with excitement. Though technically Penny was under-age, she was only four years younger than him. Maybe he stood a chance with her.

For a moment, Ken gazed across Penny and watched the view from the window of the bus.

'No. I'm not a dirty old man,' Ken said. 'After all, I'm not all that much older than you. I'm eighteen. I wouldn't call that old. And I don't wear a mackintosh and I'd always thought that mackintoshes were stock in trade with dirty old men.'

Penny giggled.

'Also, I've never been keen to end up on the pages of the *News of the World*,' Ken continued. 'But I will confess one thing to you.'

'What's that?'

'If we were alone on a desert island together,' Ken said, 'I wouldn't rate your chances as being good.'

Penny laughed. 'How do you know I'd be willing?' she asked, squeezing Ken's arm.

Ken felt his body responding to Penny's touch. He smiled slowly at her. 'If you weren't willing ...' he began.

Penny wriggled in her seat. 'Oh, I see,' she said. 'I wouldn't have a great deal of say in the matter.'

Ken moved uncomfortably in his seat. His trousers seemed

suddenly unbearably tight. He longed to ease the constriction around his crotch.·

'S'pose you could say that,' he said.

'Well, you're not going to get the chance.'

'I know,' Ken said. 'That's just what I want to try and explain to you. I promise, I won't so much as lay a finger on you. I feel happy being with you. That's no crime.'

Ken became aware of the pressure of Penny's knee against his leg. He looked across at her. She smiled sweetly at him.

'Tell me, Penny, what are you doing tomorrow afternoon?' Ken asked.

'Nothing special,' Penny replied. 'Why?'

'I was wondering if you'd like to go to the pictures with me,' Ken enquired.

'I don't mind,' Penny said. 'I'm sure I can come up with some suitable excuse for my mother.' She thought for a moment. 'I know. I can tell her I'm going over to my friend Hilary for the afternoon.'

Ken smiled broadly. 'It's a date, then?' he asked.

Penny nodded her head. 'Yes,' she said. 'Where shall we meet?'

'What about outside the Station Hotel in Putney High Street?' Ken suggested.

'That's fine by me. What time?'

'Two o'clock?'

'Great,' Penny agreed. 'And I know there's a new Bette Davis film showing. *Jezebel*. I really want to see it.'

The bus was pulling into their stop. Ken stood up and stepped back to allow Penny to get out of the seat and move down the stairs in front of him.

'You won't let me down, will you?' Ken asked anxiously, as they stood on the pavement. Pedestrians hurried past them.

'Course not, silly,' Penny said. 'I must go now.'

The girl smiled up at Ken and then turned away and began to walk up the road. 'See you tomorrow,' she called turning back towards him. She waved, then moved briskly off and disappeared around the corner.

The following day Ken was up early. He shaved carefully,

cursing his dark beard. Then he gave himself a thorough wash. Once his father had left for work, Ken asked his mother to press his best grey flannels. He polished his shoes until they gleamed. Dressed in his freshly pressed flannels, a crisply starched white shirt, and his polished brogues, Ken set off for his meeting with Penny. He knew that he would be early, even if he walked slowly. But his excitement was such that he knew he couldn't sit around at home until it was time to leave. Once he reached the Station Hotel, Ken realised that he had a good half-an-hour to wait. He decided to go into the public bar and have a pint of bitter while he waited. He felt nervous and edgy and feared that perhaps Penny wouldn't keep her date with him.

At five minutes to two Ken was standing outside the pub. Nervously he peered up and down the street; he watched each bus as it pulled into the stop and intently examined each dismounting passenger. When Penny arrived, a few minutes past the hour, he breathed a sigh of relief.

'I'm sorry I'm a bit late,' she said in apology. 'I had to wait an age for the bus.'

'That's all right,' Ken said. 'You're here. That's all that matters.'

They walked off towards the cinema.

Romantic drama wasn't Ken's idea of an entertaining film at the best of times, and his closeness to Penny made it even more difficult for him to concentrate on it. He noticed that the girl was entranced, her eyes rarely left the screen. Yet it was apparent that Penny was far from oblivious to his presence. Her slender body leaned casually against him and more than once her knee pressed lightly against his. Ken rested an arm lightly around Penny's shoulders.

As the film ended, Ken and Penny stood up to leave the cinema.

'Gosh, that was good,' Penny breathed excitedly. Her eyes sparkled with pleasure.

Ken and Penny walked up the aisle and out into the foyer.

'Didn't you think Bette Davis was wonderful?' Penny asked.

Ken wasn't sure what to say. He paused for a moment,

trying to remember his impressions of the film.

'I thought she was a bit hard,' he mumbled shyly.

'What about Henry Fonda?' Penny asked. 'Didn't you think he was good-looking?'

'If I'd thought he was good-looking,' Ken said, 'I wouldn't be here with you.'

Penny giggled. 'You know,' she said, 'I think you look a bit like Henry Fonda.'

Ken preened himself. 'Do you really?' he asked. 'Do you think *I'd* make a good film star?'

They were standing outside the cinema, now, and the crowds ebbed and flowed about them. Unexpectedly, Penny took Ken's arm and squeezed it.

'Oh, yes,' she breathed. 'I think you're ever so handsome.'

They began to walk away from the cinema.

'What do you want to do now?' Ken asked.

'Well,' Penny said after a pause, 'I told my mother that I would be at Hilary's until quite late. I don't have to be home until ten.'

'How about a walk, then?' Ken suggested. 'It's a lovely afternoon.'

Penny nodded. 'That sounds like a nice idea,' she agreed.

They walked in silence for a while, up Putney Hill in the general direction of the Common.

'Do you often go riding on the Common?' Ken asked suddenly.

'When I can,' Penny said. 'But how did you know that I went riding?'

Ken blushed. 'I saw you there once,' he admitted. 'I hoped I'd see you again and I couldn't believe my luck when I ran into you yesterday afternoon.'

Penny grinned up at him. 'You are funny,' she said. 'There's nothing special about me.'

Ken detected a teasing tone in Penny's voice. 'Maybe there isn't,' he said.

Covertly, Ken watched Penny's face. The smile began to fade.

'Maybe there isn't,' he repeated. 'Not for everyone. But

there certainly is for me. You're the prettiest girl I've ever seen.'

'Flatterer,' Penny said, smiling with pleasure. 'But I thank you just the same for your kind words.'

By now they were walking on the grass of the Common.

'Gosh, I feel puffed,' Penny said. 'Let's sit down for a bit and have a rest.'

'Don't mind if I do,' Ken agreed.

'Let's head for the shade of the trees,' Penny suggested. 'It will be nice and cool there ... and no one will be able to see us.'

For a few minutes more they walked through the long grass towards a sheltered spot. Penny seemed to be leading the way, following a rough track as if she were already familiar with it.

'Been here before?' Ken asked with a conspiratorial wink.

'A friend of my mother's owns horses, and he and I always used to ride to this spot,' Penny explained. 'He used to give me riding lessons. This track leads to a quiet clearing and we always used to go there for a rest.'

Ken let Penny lead him towards a small clearing, sheltered by the towering trees, with grass and leaves beneath their feet and so quiet that even the sound of the birds seemed to have been stilled.

'This is the life,' Ken said, stretching his arms.

Penny flopped down onto the grass. Ken sat down beside her. He stared down at her slender form, at the face with its curious mixture of innocence and sensuality, at the blonde hair spread out like a fan on the grass behind her head. Penny smiled.

'Like it here?' she asked.

Ken nodded. He took a cigarette from his packet and lit it. He smoked in silence.

'Can I have a drag?' Penny asked.

'Aren't you a bit young to be smoking?'

Penny shook her head. 'Dave always used to let me have a drag on his cigarette,' she said.

'Who's this Dave?' Ken asked.

'My riding master,' Penny told him.

'And how old was he?'

'Oh, very mature,' Penny said. 'About forty, I should think. Now, can I have a drag on your ciggie?'

Ken passed his cigarette to Penny, she dragged expertly on it and then exhaled smoke.

'It's quiet here,' Ken murmured.

Penny gazed up at him through half-closed eyes. 'Yes,' she said softly. 'That's why Dave liked it.'

Ken felt a stab of excitement in his stomach. He eased himself back down beside Penny, resting himself on his side with his chin cupped in the palm of his hand.

'You're a knowing little thing, aren't you?' he said slowly. His voice seemed to have become very thick, as if the words couldn't quite get by his tongue.

Penny smiled lazily. She let one hand rise in the air and then fall gently across one of her small, barely formed breasts.

'If you say so,' she said.

Shyly, Ken inclined himself forward. He kissed Penny on the forehead.

'My riding master said the horses were sweating, so we must stop for a while,' Penny told him in a dreamy voice. 'I was just fourteen. He tied the reins to the branch of a tree and we sat on this very bank sharing one of his cigarettes.'

Ken listened to the girl speaking, but the words seemed indistinct, not registering completely in his mind. His awareness of the girl sprawled out beside him was numbing every sense in his body. His nostrils seemed to be full of the smell of lavender water and sweat which drifted up from Penny's body. His eyes could see only the small breasts, the arms and legs, the blonde hair. Her words came to him as a blur of sound.

Penny presented a picture of complete trust and innocence which was so beautiful to Ken that at that instant he felt a stab of pain for all of it that would be destroyed in the years to come. At that instant – for the first time in his life – perhaps for the only time in his life – Ken supposed he knew what people meant when they talked about 'pure love'. He wasn't even tempted to touch the girl. He was happy simply to gaze down at the slim body and the softness of the skin of her face.

'I was lying here,' Penny continued slowly, 'and Dave came and lay down beside me. It was very warm in the wood and very quiet. We might have been the only people in it. He touched me, very softly at first. Here and here.'

Ken watched fascinated as Penny slowly placed a hand on each breast. The fingers of each hand spread out and completely covered her breasts. For a moment the hands were completely still; then Penny began to rub her breasts gently.

'At first, I hardly noticed what Dave was doing,' Penny continued. 'But then I could feel my body stirring. It was as if an electric current was going through me. I began to get more excited than I'd ever been in my life. I didn't even think about stopping him when he started to unbutton my blouse.'

Penny paused. She stared at Ken.

The cigarette in his hand had burnt down completely. Ken tossed the stub into the undergrowth. As he moved, he became aware of a constriction in his crotch and an unbelievable ache in his balls.

'So you see,' Penny said. 'You needn't worry.'

As Ken watched, Penny slowly began to unbutton her blouse.

'I knew what you wanted when you started to talk to me at the bus stop,' Penny said. Her face was now flushed and her fingers stumbled feverishly over the buttons. 'I knew what you wanted ... and I wanted the same.'

Penny reached out and took Ken's hand in her own. She guided Ken's hand inside the opened blouse and placed it over a breast.

'Touch me there,' she said, and moved the hand. 'And there.'

Ken felt his mind reeling with excitement, with shock, with a sense of unbelief.

Penny's skirt had ridden up to expose her thighs. She moved his hand from her breasts and placed it on a thigh.

Ken began stroking.

'And here,' Penny moaned. 'Touch me *here*.'

5

Ken stopped speaking; he raised his head and looked across at Paul, who was stretched out on the sand.

'From that instant, there was no going back,' Ken continued. 'I was like a thing possessed. I had to see her every day.'

Paul nodded. 'I understand,' he said softly. 'But what then was wrong with that?'

Ken unclasped his hands, he lifted them palms upwards and stared down at them as if they might hold the answer to some awful problem.

'It couldn't work,' he said. 'She was under-age. She was only fourteen.'

Ken stood up and began to pace back and forth along the sand.

'I was a fool. I should have known something would go wrong. It was too good to be true. You see, she wanted it as much as me. Sex was like a drug to her – and she got me hooked. That innocent face was just a mask. She was as randy as hell. God! That riding master had taught her every trick in the book.'

Ken turned abruptly and glared at Paul.

'What I was doing was a criminal offence. It didn't matter a jot or a tittle that Penny was every bit as willing as me. To the Law she was a minor.'

'Ken, calm down,' Paul murmured. 'Don't be so angry. Explain. I don't understand.'

Ken flung himself down on the sand. 'Give me a cigarette, will you?' he asked.

Paul passed a cigarette across to Ken. For a while the two men smoked in silence.

'It couldn't last,' Ken continued. 'Something had to go wrong. She couldn't keep going out for our long afternoons without her mother wondering what was going on. One day she called Penny's friend's house. The friend's mother answered the phone. Penny's mum said that Penny and Hilary seemed to be spending a lot of time together. Well ... that blew the whole thing sky high. Because Penny hadn't seen Hilary for weeks. When she got home that night, her mother asked Penny where she'd been. Of course, Penny said that she'd been with Hilary. Her mother called her a liar. There was the most awful row. But Penny didn't say anything. Her mother accused her of seeing some boy. But Penny made various excuses. God knows what her mother was like. The following day, she dragged Penny down to the family doctor and had her examined. Then the fat *was* in the fire because obviously the doctor discovered that Penny was no longer a virgin. Her ma hit the roof.'

Ken tossed his half-finished cigarette onto the sand.

'What happened?' Paul enquired.

'Naturally, I didn't know any of this was going on,' Ken said. 'But the following afternoon, when Penny didn't turn up I got worried. I knew she was as eager to see me as I was to see her. Something serious must have cropped up to make her break our date. Like an idiot, I telephoned. Penny's mum answered the phone. She didn't sound at all friendly. I pretended to have the wrong number and hung up.'

'So how were you caught?' Paul asked.

'I was in a daze,' Ken explained. 'I behaved like a fucking idiot. I loved that girl, you know. You have to believe that. It wasn't just sex. I loved her. I had to see her again. So I did about the most stupid thing you could imagine. I wrote to Penny.'

Paul shook his head. 'And her mother opened the letter?' he said.

Ken gave an ironic laugh. 'You've got it in one,' he said. 'Her mother read the letter and realised what had been going on, and called the police. The reply to my letter wasn't the one I'd expected. I came home one evening and my mum told me the police had been round asking about me. They came back that night. I was dragged off down to the station. It wasn't pleasant, I can tell you. They got the truth out of me, all right. And along the way they turned something that had been special and important into something dirty.'

There was a look of hatred in Ken's dark eyes.

'They treated me like shit,' he said angrily. 'They made me feel like the worst kind of pervert. There was nothing I could say.'

'What about the girl?' Paul asked. 'Penny?'

'Bless her,' Ken said. 'She stood up for me. Said that she'd agreed to everything; said she'd encouraged me. She told them that we were in love. But it didn't make a blind bit of difference. I was charged. They treat sex with under-age girls as "Unlawful Intercourse", you see. I was sent for trial. There was no hope for it. In Court, Penny's mother swore that Penny was an innocent who had been seduced by an evil man. Penny had been dressed up in her school uniform – and, my God, she looked about twelve and as though butter wouldn't melt in her mouth. I didn't stand a chance. I was sent down.'

'Sent down?' Paul asked.

'Sent to prison,' Ken said. 'An experience I'd rather forget.'

'What about Penny?'

'She was all right, of course, because she was a minor. Though I bet that mother of hers gave her real hell,' Ken said gloomily. 'I realised, though, that by the time I came out of jug, my darling Penny would have found another man. I'm not complaining, understand. What I regret, though, is the moment when I first looked down at her in that glade. When I loved her. I'll never feel like that again.'

Paul's face was full of concern and sympathy. 'You don't know that, Ken,' he said gently.

'What do you know about it?' Ken replied irritably.

'Ken ...' Paul began.

But Ken interrupted him, his temper flaring in a sudden flash of anger. 'All right. I've told you,' he cried out. 'What more do you want? Blood?'

A look of hurt crossed Paul's face. 'Ken ...' he said, changing the subject, 'what will you do when the war is finished?'

Ken smiled weakly at Paul. 'I'm sorry,' he said. 'I didn't mean to shout at you.'

'Forget it,' Paul said.

Ken walked over and patted Paul on the shoulder. 'You're a pal,' he said.

'What will you do when the war is over?' Paul repeated.

'Depends which side's won, doesn't it?' Ken answered.

'Say neither side wins,' Paul suggested. 'Say that somehow it ends in peace. What will you do?'

Ken thought for a moment. 'Set up in a garage, perhaps,' he said. 'That is, if I could find the cash. Not that I've got much chance of that, anyhow.'

'Since I've been in the army,' Paul told him, 'I've learned to be a mechanic. We could set up a garage together.'

'Preston and Seidler,' Ken said. 'Fix your old tanks in a jiffy. Tracks fitted vhile you vait.'

'While you wait,' Paul corrected smiling.

Ken spoke casually. 'Speaking of old tanks,' he said, 'do you happen to know what regiment it was that shot up your patrol last week?'

'*Ich weiss nicht*,' Paul replied.

'I ask,' Ken continued, 'because it seems odd them machine-gunning the men from your tank. In our regiment, if a man does manage to get out of a tank we've shot up, we let him be.'

'They killed every man from our tank,' Paul said.

Ken's voice was no longer casual. 'As they got out?' he asked.

'As they were getting out,' Paul answered. 'And as they were escaping.'

'You were in the Sergeant's tank?'

'Sergeant Mantner's tank. Yes,' Paul replied, moving his hands uneasily.

'And all three men were killed?'

'Yes!' Paul shouted suddenly. 'Please, Ken ... *Genug* ... Enough.'

'I'm sorry ...' Ken began. Then he stopped and slowly shook his head.

There was a moment of silence.

'What is it?' Paul asked.

'I just don't believe you,' Ken answered quietly. 'That's all.'

There was a slight tremor in Paul's voice when he spoke. 'I give you my word,' he said.

'All three men were stone dead when you left?'

'Yes,' Paul answered defiantly.

'One of them wasn't just wounded?' Ken suggested.

'No,' Paul stated.

'You checked?' Ken asked.

'*Natürlich.*'

'While the bullets swept over you?'

'While your tanks followed our two Mark Threes,' Paul explained.

'You're a gunner,' Ken said. 'At what range can you knock out a Crusader?'

'With our seventy-five? At one thousand two hundred metres,' Paul replied. 'Easily.'

'Well, our two-pounder can't knock you out till we close to eight hundred. So what's all this about chasing?' Ken asked.

'I have not say "chase",' Paul answered stubbornly. 'I said "followed". Besides, your Crusaders move faster than we can. And we were outnumbered.'

Ken looked coldly across at Paul; for an instant he remained silent.

'No garage,' Ken said flatly.

Paul looked confused. '*Bitte?*' he asked.

'I'm not going into partnership with someone who lies to me,' Ken said speaking deliberately slowly.

Paul stood up and for a moment looked down at Ken. He

then walked to his bivouac and sat down to read his book. He
looked up, peering over the cover of the book.

'You call me a liar?' he asked.

'Yes,' Ken answered. 'Why not?'

For a minute there was silence. Ken stood up and walked
over to the tank. He hoisted himself onto the body of the
machine.

'Pity the tank wireless is busted,' Ken said. 'On those
number nine sets you can pick up the BBC. And there's
nothing more heartening than to hear that you're advancing
steadily with two prongs in a pincer attack, when you know
you've just fled for your life for the last three days.'

Ken stopped speaking and looked towards Paul. The
German seemed to be reading intently.

'Terribly keen on prongs and pincers is the BBC,' Ken
continued. 'I reckon their military expert is a retired
surgeon ... "A firm incision has been made in the enemy
lines ... Mopping-up operations are now in progress ... Our
troops have now withdrawn to carefully prepared positions."
That's the nursing home stage.'

Once more, Ken looked towards Paul. But the German
ignored him. Paul turned over a page of his book and
continued to read intently.

'Come on,' Ken said jovially. 'I don't care if you ran away.'

Paul's head jerked up. His face was flushed and angry. A
strand of blond hair had flopped onto his forehead. He glared
at Ken, then savagely threw the book onto the sand.

'I did not run away,' Paul shouted.

Ken smiled. 'I thought that would get you,' he said. 'Then
what *did* happen?'

Paul's face was grim.

'All right,' he said. 'The tank was hit twice. The first shot
hit the driver's compartment and killed Hans: he was our
driver. The second shot set the engine on fire. Sergeant
Mantner gave the order to abandon tank and run for it. First
he got out of the turret. Then the wireless-operator. Then it
was my turn. There was some machine-gun fire – but not
much. When I got to the ground I saw that Mantner and

Klaus, the wireless-operator, were running to the west. Klaus
had been wounded in the arm – but not badly. When I began
to run I stumbled and fell. I was dazed, I think, by the noise of
our gun and by the shells crashing against our tank. But in a
second I was up on my feet again ... I saw Mantner and Klaus
disappearing to the west ... Your Crusader tanks had swept to
the north ... For a moment at least I was alone ... And I began
running ... But I ran to the south.'

'Why?' Ken asked. 'Why south?'

'I wanted to be by myself for a time,' Paul stated.

'Because you were afraid?' Ken said. 'Because you'd lost
your nerve?'

'Because I wanted to get away from him,' Paul said
reluctantly.

'Get away from who?' Ken asked.

There was silence for a moment.

'Mantner,' Paul replied hesitantly. 'Sergeant Mantner. The
tank crews of your side also, I think, must sleep beside their
tank.'

'Yes.'

'Sometimes we sleep in one bivouac. Sometimes in small
tents.'

Ken nodded.

'Sergeant Mantner ordered it so that I shared a tent with
him,' Paul told Ken, speaking in a voice without emotion. 'At
first I thought it would be all right.'

Paul turned away from Ken and stared out across the
desert. He sat very still, without speaking. His attention
seemed far away, his concentration focused on the black mass
of the desert dimly perceived through the dark of the night.

'I had seen him looking at me,' Paul continued with a
struggle, still gazing away from Ken. 'But I thought my
suspicion was wrong. Then, after we had been in the desert for
some weeks, one night he tried. But ... I would not. And after
a short time ... he gave up.'

Paul swivelled round again and faced Ken. His blue eyes
still seemed to be focused elsewhere.

'But the next day Mantner began picking on me,' Paul said

in a quiet voice. 'If there was any specially hard work to be done, I was chosen to do it. If anything went wrong, I was blamed. If there was an extra guard duty round the tanks, I did it. And each night, though never obviously, each night he would somehow let me know what it was he wanted. So, when the chance came, I went south. Now do you understand?'

Sitting on the tank, Ken started down at Paul. He ran his fingers through the curls of his hair. He shook his head.

'I don't know about your side. But if that happened to one of our men, he'd have two alternatives,' Ken said slowly. 'He could report it to his troop leader, his officer – or he could ask to be transferred to another tank, without giving an exact reason.'

'Well, it is not so with us,' Paul announced bitterly.

'Do you mean a German soldier can't complain if his Sergeant tries ...?'

'No, I tell you. No,' Paul replied.

Ken swung himself down from the tank. He looked sullen. 'No garage,' he said.

Paul stared at him in surprise. '*Bitte*?' he asked.

'I'm not going into business with someone who tells me lies.'

'Ken, it is the truth I have told you,' Paul said. There was a note of pleading in his voice.

'Parts of the truth, maybe,' Ken stated. 'Not all of it by any means.'

'*Du bist ein Idiot*,' Paul shouted at him. 'You are an idiot.'

'Sometimes,' Ken agreed affably. 'But not right now.'

'I have not lied to you,' Paul said in a quieter voice.

'I believe most of it – so far as it goes. It's simply that I have a feeling there's something you've left out.'

'What?' Paul asked. 'What could I have left out?'

Ken spoke slowly. 'You know that better than me,' he said.

Paul shook his head.

'You could have left out the reason you didn't even think of complaining to someone,' Ken suggested.

Paul turned away from him. 'Why should I care what you think?' he demanded.

'Exactly!' Ken replied. 'Why indeed?'

Paul turned back and stared straight at Ken. 'All right,' he said. 'My father is not the manager of an hotel – as I tell people – but only an assistant clerk in the office.'

'Who cares?'

Paul clenched his fists together at his sides. 'Sergeant Mantner also comes from Riesbach,' he said.

'Well, so what? Everyone comes from somewhere,' Ken acknowledged.

Paul took a step forward. 'But he could say things – to people – in Riesbach,' he said.

'Let him.'

Paul's eyes were glittering with rage. 'You're lucky, Kenneth Preston, with your motorbike and your father in the bank and your little girl in the woods,' he said bitterly.

'What?' Ken shouted angrily. '*What* was that you said?'

Nervously Paul looked across at Ken. 'Sorry,' he muttered. 'I didn't mean it. I just couldn't help it.'

The tension of anger relaxed from Ken's face. 'For a man on the run, you certainly take a load of risks,' he said.

'I'm not on the run,' Paul protested. 'But I am running.'

He sat down on the upturned ammunition box. He took a cigarette from his packet and lit it. For a few moments, Paul sucked contemplatively on his cigarette.

When he spoke again, his voice was resigned. 'So you want to know about me, Ken Preston,' he said slowly. 'All right, I will tell you.'

Ken walked across to Paul and took a cigarette from the packet. He then sat down in the canvas chair.

'I'm all ears,' he said.

'In the last war my father was a simple soldier,' Paul began, 'but he thought himself an officer. I must stand up when he came into the room. I must not speak unless I am spoken to. From as far back as I can remember, I hated him. When I was fifteen, I had been out with friends for once. My father had told me to be in early. But I was late. When I came in he was waiting for me.'

6

Hermann Seidler looked up as Paul came in, closing the door to the street quietly. He was late. Seidler extracted his pocket-watch from his waistcoat and stared down at it. Paul was very late, the boy had no discipline, no respect. Seidler listened to the sounds from the small hallway. He heard Paul remove his coat and hang it in the cupboard. He heard the door close.

Seidler pushed his chair back from the table and stood up. Though he was not a tall man, Hermann Seidler was imposing. His stomach stuck out in front of him, and his shirt seemed tightly stretched across his barrel-chest. Yet his upright military bearing made him seem taller than he was. It was a warm evening and he had removed his jacket. His shirt sleeves were neatly rolled to his elbows, the buttons of his waistcoat were undone.

Hermann Seidler lifted the stein of lager to his lips and took a series of gulps from it. He wiped the foam from the short bristles of his moustache. His face was red, with small broken veins across his florid cheeks.

'Paul!' he called in a voice of harsh command.

The door opened and Paul entered the room nervously. He looked small and frail in the soft light from the reading lamp.

'Sir?' Paul asked hesitantly.

Seidler swung the watch in front of him and with a deft movement caught it in the palm of his hand. He peered down as if to examine the face.

'What time is it?' he demanded.

'I don't know, sir,' Paul said standing stiffly to attention.

'You don't know?' Seidler roared. 'Why don't you know?'

'I'm sorry, sir,' Paul murmured. 'I must have forgotten the time.'

'It is after nine o'clock,' his father bellowed. 'You are extremely late in getting back. The *Jugendbewegung* meeting has been over for some time. What have you been up to?'

Paul could feel his hands beginning to tremble. He shook his head. 'Nothing, sir,' he responded.

'Nothing?' Seidler repeated with a sneer. 'We'll see about this nothing. You know the rules? You understand what happens when you disobey them?'

Paul nodded his head unhappily. 'I understand,' he said.

'Then go to your room,' his father commanded. 'I will come up shortly.'

Paul inclined his head towards his father. 'Yes, sir,' he said softly.

He turned and left the room, closing the door carefully behind him.

Hermann Seidler stared after his son. He sat down again at the table and raised the stein of lager. He took a long drink. A loaf of black bread and a piece of sausage were on plates on the table at his elbow. He tore off a hunk of bread and carved a thick slice of sausage. He chewed greedily on the food.

In front of him Seidler had a large book with the pages open to a place about halfway through. He read for a moment. As he finished chewing, Seidler slammed the book shut and stood up.

'The Führer is right,' he muttered to himself. 'There is too much decadence. There is not enough discipline. I will teach him respect.'

He carried the book over to a small bookcase and returned it to the shelf. He considered *Mein Kampf* to be an almost sacred book. For a moment he stood completely still, gazing at the framed photograph of Adolf Hitler which hung on the wall above the bookcase. He raised his arm in a salute.

'*Heil Hitler,*' he said and moved towards the door.

Paul listened to the sound of his father climbing heavily up the narrow stairway. He knew that already he would be unfastening his thick leather belt. Paul shivered. The night seemed suddenly to have become cold.

The door to his small and sparsely furnished room opened.

'Good. I see you are ready,' his father said, gazing down at the shivering figure now dressed only in undershorts.

As his father entered the room, Paul stood up and snapped smartly to attention.

'You are a coward, eh?' Seidler asked, noticing that Paul was trembling.

'I feel a little cold, sir,' Paul murmured.

'You will be feeling more than a little cold when I finish with you,' his father exclaimed angrily.

Paul stared at the thick belt twisted in his father's hands.

'That I should have spawned a son who is a coward and a liar!' his father shouted. 'I who have fought for the Fatherland. You are no better than a milksop. You are softer than a crawling Jewish *Schwein*. I cannot believe that you are a son of mine!'

As if it had life of its own, the belt uncoiled and hung limply at his father's side.

'Kneel,' Seidler commanded. 'At least try to take your punishment like a man.'

Paul knelt by the side of his bed, facing away from his father his chest leaning towards the counterpane. He waited for the first blow and as the belt lashed across his back he winced. He gritted his teeth and let the tears start to his eyes. But he did not cry out.

'You will learn to obey,' his father shouted. And the belt met his skin for the second time. Red weals appeared on the skin of his back. The blows continued to fall.

Much later, Paul sat on his bed listening to the sound of his father's snores coming from the room next door. How he hated him. He wondered – as he had wondered so many times before – why his mother had ever married such a brutal man.

Paul stood up and walked across to the wardrobe which contained his clothes. He reached up and pulled a battered cardboard suitcase from the top. He blew the dust from the case and opened it. Quietly he began to take garments from their hangers and fold them neatly into the case. He moved with extreme caution and as silently as he could manage. When the suitcase was full Paul dressed himself. His back stung and it was almost more than he could bear to have the fabric of his vest pressing against the weals caused by the blows from the belt.

He moved across to the bedroom door, opened it a fraction and listened. His father continued to snore. Bedsprings creaked as his mother moved restlessly in her sleep. Paul pulled the door open and tiptoed down the passage and down the stairs. He made for the kitchen. He would need food. On the scrubbed wooden table in the middle of the room was a block of cheese, a piece of sausage and the remains of a loaf of bread. Paul hunted around for a cloth or some greaseproof paper to wrap the cheese and sausage in.

He stopped guiltily. He had heard a creak from the stairs. He turned to face the door as it was pushed slowly open.

'What are you doing, Paulie?' his mother asked.

Paul breathed a sigh of relief. 'I am leaving, Mother,' he said. 'I cannot bear it here any longer.'

Frau Seidler looked at Paul in silence. Her face was filled with love and sympathy. 'I understand,' she said. 'But it will not be easy. Is your mind made up so firmly?'

Paul nodded.

Frau Seidler advanced into the room. 'I heard him again tonight," she said. 'Beating you. He is not a bad man. He is proud. I think in his own way he loves you. Yet he cannot show love, only brutality.'

'It is no good, Mother,' Paul stated. 'I must go away from here.'

Frau Seidler nodded. 'Where will you go? How will you live?'

'I shall make for Berlin,' Paul told her. 'I should be able to find work there.'

'But you have no money.'

'I will manage, Mother,' Paul said gently.

Frau Seidler moved quickly across the kitchen. She lifted the lid from a big stoneware flour jar.

'Wait,' she said, pushing her arm down through the flour.

Paul watched his mother.

'Here,' she said, handing him a small bundle of banknotes which she had pulled from the bottom of the jar of flour. She dusted the flour from the notes. 'This will help you until you find work.'

'Are you sure, Mother?'

'You are my son,' she said. 'Of course I am sure. I have always tried to set something by from what your father gives me. In case an emergency arose. This is just such an event as I was saving for. Take it. It is not much but I want you to have it.'

Paul smiled fondly at his mother. '*Danke,*' he said.

He kissed his mother on the cheek. 'I love you, Mother,' he said. 'But I cannot stay.'

'Go,' she said. 'Be happy.'

'*Danke.*'

'Take care of yourself in the big city,' his mother said. 'Be in touch.'

Paul slipped out of the door into the early morning light.

*

There was a holiday atmosphere in Berlin. Flags flew from the buildings; crowds milled about in the streets. The weather was perfect. Warm day followed warm day; the sky was always clear and blue. The shops were filled with expensive goods; the luxury hotels were thronged with tourists who could afford to spend their dollars and francs and pounds in the shops along the Friedrichstrasse and in the big department stores like Wetheims on the Leipziger Strasse.

The Olympic Games had finished a little over a week ago, and Germany's many wins had buoyed up the people. German athletes had beaten every nation, the Americans who had finished second were fifty-seven points behind them. The Fatherland had taken more gold and silver and bronze medals than any other nation. But Germany's triumphs were of no consolation to Paul as he walked in the shade of the trees in the Tiergarten.

He was hungry and tired and depressed. He had been in Berlin for three weeks now and still had not been able to find work of any kind. However menial the job, papers were needed. Paul did not have papers. His situation seemed to be hopeless. Rooms were expensive. Even the tiny room he had taken in the Hallesches Tor district cost him more than he could really afford. His landlady was well-meaning, but she was poor and the meagre meals she provided weren't appetising. Each morning, Paul had a breakfast of black bread covered with a thin scraping of butter and a cup of weak coffee; his evening meal usually consisted of watery cabbage soup and more black bread. A piece of sausage or a hunk of cheese seemed like an unimaginable luxury.

Paul had arrived in Berlin a few days before the opening of the Games. He had been excited to watch the parade which preceded the opening ceremony. Crushed into the enormous crowd, Paul watched as the long procession, led by the Führer, had moved down the ten miles of the Via Triumphalis. The crowds had gone wild with excitement – though forty-thousand Brownshirts along the route had made sure they didn't get out of control. But the excitement of those first days in Berlin was soon dissipated by pangs of hunger and moments of despair and loneliness or even home-sickness.

At first Berlin had seemed to be a magical city paved with gold; a city of opportunity. Quickly, however, Paul became disillusioned. Work was scarce and his money was beginning to run out. He would spend his days walking the streets, watching the people, admiring the many fine buildings. His favourite walk took him down the Friedrichstrasse until it bisected the Unter den Linden. He would then walk slowly down the Unter den Linden towards the Armoury and the Imperial Palace. At the Schlossplatz he would turn and, after gazing at the Palace for a while, walk slowly back down the opposite side of the Unter den Linden towards the Tiergarten. The broad, elegant street looking away down towards the

Brandenburg Gate always inspired him with a sense of power and majesty and he would meander along slowly past the Adlon Hotel and the British Embassy and, eventually, pass beneath the columns at the side of the Brandenburg Gate into the green calmness of the Tiergarten.

This walk led Paul past imposing buildings and people who appeared to have enough leisure and money to enjoy themselves. The way of life he observed on these streets made a sharp contrast to his own way of living; he enjoyed standing outside the Adlon watching the entrances and exits of beautiful women and elegant men, of Army officers and of officers of the S.S. in their black uniforms with silver flashes and highly polished boots. It was a world he knew he would not be able to enter, yet he felt no envy, only a kind of sad longing and a regret that his life was not easier.

As he walked aimlessly through the Tiergarten, cutting across past the Rosengarten down towards the river, Paul became aware of a man who appeared to be following him. He continued to move casually towards the Luther Bridge, sensing that the man was still behind him and walking in the same direction. When he reached the river, Paul turned and began to stroll back in the direction of the Brandenburg Gate, skirting along the path which followed the Spree. He stopped for a while and gazed down at the waters of the river. He noticed that the man had stopped too and that he also was watching the river.

Paul moved on. He walked slowly, stopping occasionally – on the pretext of admiring the view, of having to re-tie the laces of his shoe. Each time he ceased to move, the man behind him would slow down or stop. In one instance, the man moved a little ahead of Paul before sitting down on a wooden bench. Once Paul started to move again, the man stood up and continued to follow him.

As they neared the Brandenburg Gate, Paul decided to sit down on one of the wooden benches and see what the man did. He paused to read a wooden sign. Underneath the words '*Bank für Juden dort*' was an arrow painted in red which indicated a bench where Jews could sit. The sign was freshly painted; it had not been there a few days ago. But then Paul knew that most of the evident indications of the National Socialists' anti-Semitism had been tactfully removed whilst the Games had been on. *Der Stürmer*, the passionately anti-Jewish newspaper edited by Julius Streicher which his father back in Riesbach read so avidly, had disappeared from the newspaper kiosks. Paul knew that one or two Jews had actually represented the Reich in the Games; though one of them had shot himself after he had been replaced by a true German.

Paul knew that his father hated the Jews; no term of abuse was strong enough when he ranted and raved about them. Many evenings when he had been at home his father would expound on the evils of the world conspiracy of Jews and the menace of the Jewish doctrine of communism which was spreading like a blight across the world. Paul couldn't really understand his father's attitude; he remembered that until a few years ago his father had used the Jewish tailor in Riesbach, always saying how good he was. Paul himself had had a Jewish friend when he was at Kindergarten. But now everything was different. Jews were the cause of all the problems which beset the Reich, he heard on the wireless and read in the newspapers. Perhaps he was just too young or to stupid, as his father would say, to understand.

He noticed that the man who had been following him was approaching the bench upon which he had sat. The man came level with Paul.

'Do you mind if I sit here?' he asked.

Paul shook his head. The man sat down a little way along the bench from Paul. He took a packet of Salem Aleikum cigarettes from the pocket of his jacket and lit one. Paul sniffed in the pungent odour of the Turkish tobacco.

'Would you like one?' the man said, extending the packet towards Paul.

Paul took a cigarette. '*Danke*,' he said.

The man moved closer towards Paul. He struck a match and held it out towards Paul's cigarette.

Paul noticed that the man's fingers were long and thin, like a musician's, and that his nails were neatly manicured and highly polished.

'You don't look very happy,' the man said.

Paul puffed on his cigarette.

'Do you have a job of work?' the man asked.

Paul shook his head. 'No,' he said. 'Work is hard to find. I had not thought it would be so difficult.'

Paul looked at the man. He had a kind face, long and thin. His eyes were dark but warm and when he smiled his face expressed a lively and alert look which suggested a gentle sense of humour. Of course, he was old. He looked as if he were about forty, as old as his hated father.

'When did you last eat?' the man asked.

'Breakfast. This morning.'

'Ah,' the man said, nodding his head. 'And what did that consist of?'

'A cup of coffee and a piece of bread,' Paul told him.

'Not much for a growing boy.'

'No,' Paul agreed. 'But the woman with whom I lodge does her best. She cannot afford to give me more.'

'How old are you?'

'Almost sixteen.'

They were silent for a moment.

'I imagine you could do with something to eat,' the man said.

Paul remembered his meagre breakfast. He thought about the inevitable cabbage soup which would be provided for his dinner that evening. After a moment, he nodded.

The man smiled at him. 'I thought so!' he exclaimed. 'Perhaps you would allow me to buy you a meal?'

'I don't know ...' Paul began hesitantly.

'You are hungry? Yes?' the man said. 'Come with me. I will buy you a meal which will make you forget your hunger.'

It could do no harm, Paul thought. Though he was well aware that men did not approach boys they did not know and offer to buy them meals without wanting something in exchange, Paul felt he could handle any such problems which might arise. At worst, after he had finished his food, he could always run away.

'I would like that very much,' Paul said.

The man stood up. 'Good. That is settled,' he said. 'Shall we go?'

Paul stood up and they began to walk out of the gardens. As they walked, the man introduced himself.

'My name is Rolf Hagen,' he said. 'And who are you?'

'Paul. Paul Seidler,' Paul told him.

Rolf smiled at Paul. 'I am happy to make your acquaintance, Paul Seidler,' he said.

They had turned off the Unter den Linden by now. At a cross street, Paul paused for a moment and gazed into the window of a shop which sold sheet music, gramophone records and musical instruments.

'What has caught your eye, Paul?' Rolf asked.

'There,' Paul said, pointing into the shop window.

Rolf peered into the window. 'The *Mundharmonika*?' he asked.

'Yes,' Paul said. 'The mouth-organ. Is it not beautiful?'

'You would like it?' Rolf asked.

Paul gazed wistfully at the mouth-organ. 'Yes,' he said. 'But I could never afford it.'

Rolf smiled at Paul. At that instant he looked very happy.

'Then you shall have it,' Rolf said. 'You will permit me to buy it for you?'

'I couldn't,' Paul protested.

'It would make me happy to give it to you as a present,' Rolf said. 'Then we will be friends.'

Paul looked again into the shop window at the mouth-organ. He felt an overwhelming desire to possess it. He nodded his head.

'Thank you,' he said. 'I would like that very much.'

'Wait here,' Rolf said. 'I will not be a minute.'

He disappeared into the dim interior of the shop. Paul watched through the window as an assistant came forward. Rolf spoke and pointed towards the display. The assistant moved forward and took the mouth-organ from the window. A few moments later, Rolf was outside. He handed to Paul the small, brown-paper wrapped package he was carrying.

'*Danke*,' Paul said, grinning. 'I don't know how to thank you. I shall treasure this. Always.'

'Don't say another word,' Rolf said. 'The look on your face is thanks enough. Now, come. We must find somewhere to eat.'

At the corner of the Friedrichstrasse and the Taubenstrasse Rolf led Paul into a restaurant.

'I think this will do us nicely,' he said. 'The Patzenhofer is really rather good. I think they are even mentioned in some of the guide books.'

'Isn't it rather grand?' Paul asked, staring around him.

Rolf laughed. 'Not at all,' he said. 'It is a good German beer restaurant. We should be able to get something substantial here at a reasonable cost ... and the beer will be excellent.'

Once they were seated and had ordered a meal – much to Rolf's amusement Paul had requested thick lentil soup to start with, boiled corned pig's knuckle with sauerkraut and mashed potato to follow, and chocolate cake after that – they began to talk.

'Is it good?' Rolf asked, watching as Paul took a long gulp of his beer and started to spoon up the thick spicy soup.

Paul nodded his head enthusiastically. 'Yes,' he said, breaking off a piece of bread from the roll on the plate to the side of his bowl of soup.

'Tell me about yourself,' Rolf said. 'How do you come to be in Berlin?'

Paul finished his soup and pushed the empty bowl away from him. The waiter served him with a steaming plate of meat and vegetables.

'I come from Riesbach,' Paul began. 'But life there was unbearable. I had to get away.'

'Didn't you get on with your family?' Rolf asked.

Paul paused for a moment, a forkful of food poised on the way to his mouth. A look of sadness crossed his face. He lowered the fork and rested it on the plate.

'Perhaps I should not ask so personal a question?' Rolf suggested.

'No. It is all right,' Paul answered. 'I got on with my mother. She is a good woman. She has always done her best for us and tried to make a happy home.'

'But you didn't get on with your father?'

'I hate my father,' Paul said with sudden vehemence. 'I hate him.'

Rolf took a drink from his stein of beer. 'Why?' he asked gently. 'Why do you hate your father?'

'He is a bully,' Paul began. 'He is without any kindness or love.'

As he ate his food, Paul told Rolf about his life in Riesbach, about the endless beatings from his father, about the unbearably strict discipline, about the atmosphere of brutality which hung about his father like clouds surrounding a mountain peak. Rolf listened in silence.

'So, you see,' Paul concluded, 'I simply could not stay there any longer.'

'I understand,' Rolf said.

'My mother gave me what money she could spare,' Paul told him. 'It was enough to get me to Berlin and enough to get me a room in a poor neighbourhood. But I did not think things would be so difficult. I cannot find work.'

Paul stopped speaking. He looked across the table at Rolf. Suddenly he felt safe with this man; he knew that Rolf would do nothing to hurt him. He smiled softly.

'I do not have papers,' Paul confided. 'So it is impossible to get a job.'

Rolf whistled softly. 'That would make things difficult,' he said.

'Sometimes I wonder what on earth I can do,' Paul blurted out. 'My mind feels like it will explode with the worry of trying to find an answer to my problems.'

Gently Rolf extended his arm across the table. He placed his hand on Paul's wrist and stroked it absent-mindedly.

'Don't worry,' he said. 'I will help you … If you will let me.'

Paul looked down at the long fingers on his wrist. The

polished nails gleamed in the light. He felt as if he were looking down at his own body from some high and distant place. Yet the fingers on his flesh were pleasantly cool and their small movements caused small palpitations from his heart. He felt safe with Rolf and yet he felt something more which he could not quite define. He felt safe and he felt some strange kind of excitement.

The waiter appeared at the side of the table. 'Is there anything more you would like?' he asked.

Rolf removed his hand and leaned back in his chair. He gazed at Paul. His look seemed to be curiously penetrating.

'Would you like coffee here?' he asked. 'Or shall we have coffee back at my apartment?'

Paul thought for a moment. He was now sure he knew what would happen if he went back with Rolf to his apartment. Yet somehow he didn't mind. He was conscious of the waiter hovering by the side of the table. Paul gazed across at Rolf. A small smile formed at the corners of his mouth. He nodded his head gently.

'Let us have coffee at your apartment, Rolf,' he said.

Once outside the restaurant, Rolf began to walk briskly towards the narrow streets of old Berlin. The fine, colonnaded buildings disappeared. The buildings became smaller, the roads were no longer wide and elegant but cramped and shadowed.

'We are almost there,' Rolf said as they turned down Kollnischestrasse.

They began to ease their pace. Just past a small row of iron railings Rolf crossed the road.

'This is it,' he said, pausing in front of a door to one side of a tobacconist's shop.

Paul looked upwards. He could see three floors above the shop. The windows directly above the shop had neat boxes of flowers outside them. From the wall a metal sign advertising '*Zigarren und Tabak*' stuck out over the street.

'Herr Weiss, who runs the shop, lives on the first floor,' Rolf pointed out as he opened the front door.

Rolf started up the staircase. 'I have a small apartment at

the top,' he said. 'When I had more money I lived in a much larger place near to the Tiergarten. But since I have been doing less work, I have less money.'

At the top of the stairs Rolf opened another door. 'Well, here we are,' he said. 'Home.'

Paul followed Rolf into a tiny entrance hall. Framed posters hung around the walls, a bentwood coat-rack stood in one corner.

'I see you are admiring my posters,' Rolf said.

Noticing Rolf's name on one of the posters, Paul turned, 'Are you an actor?' he asked.

'Yes,' Rolf said. 'Though I get little enough chance to act these days.'

He led Paul into a large and comfortably furnished sitting-room with windows which looked out onto the street. The proportions of the room were good, but it seemed to be over-crowded with furniture. Two heavy, over-stuffed sofas were set at right angles and seemed to fill the centre of the room. One wall was completely covered by shelves which overflowed with books. Another wall was covered with framed posters. One corner of the room was entirely filled by a baby grand piano, the top of which was covered entirely by photographs in silver frames.

'The piano doesn't get used much,' Rolf said. 'It belonged to a friend who used to live with me. When he went to England in 1932, he gave it to me.'

Paul was examining the photographs on the top of the piano. Coming over to stand by his side, Rolf let his arm rest lightly around Paul's shoulder.

'Bergner, Dietrich, Reinhardt, Conrad Veidt,' he said, nodding at the photographs, 'I've worked with them all.'

'Marlene Dietrich,' Paul said. 'She is a big Hollywood star.'

Rolf laughed. 'She wasn't then,' he said. 'She was just another struggling actress.'

'Are you famous?' Paul asked.

Rolf shook his head. 'Not really,' he said. 'I used to be quite well-known. But I was never a star. I am what the critics describe as "a good supporting actor".'

'Have you made films?' Paul asked.

'Yes, quite a few,' Rolf answered.

'Anything I would have seen?'

'I doubt it very much,' Rolf said. 'Now, enough of your questions for the moment. I shall go and make the coffee. Make yourself at home.'

Rolf walked through the door which led off to the kitchen.

'Do you like Turkish coffee?' he called.

'I don't know. I've never had it,' Paul answered.

'Well, there's a first time for everything,' Rolf said. 'I adore it ,.. and I hope you will, too.'

Paul heard the sound of running water and the pop as the gas was lit. Soon the strong smell of coffee began to drift into the room.

'Won't be long,' Rolf called to Paul.

Paul walked across to the wall of books and began to read the titles from the spines. Many of the books looked heavy and dull, many appeared to be scripts of plays. Some of the titles were in English, and since he had been taught English in school, he could read them. Paul noticed several titles which confirmed his suspicions about Rolf. A whole section of the bookcase seemed to be devoted to books with titles like *Die Homosexualität* (by an English writer called Havelock Ellis), *Onanie and Homosexualität* (this one by a Doktor Steckel), *Die Homosexualität des Mannes und des Weibes* (this one was also by a doctor, Doktor Magnus Hirschfeld). Further along this particular shelf were novels. Paul recognised the name of Thomas Mann. The author had been stripped of his German citizenship after refusing to return to the Fatherland from Switzerland. Paul took the slender volume from the shelf. He opened the book and began to read. He snapped the book closed and replaced it. *Der Tod in Venedig* didn't look very exciting. He selected another volume and opened it. This didn't appeal to him either. *Die Verwirrungen des Zöglings Törless* was set in a military academy and was about bullying. It reminded him of his father. Further along the shelf were more titles in English. Paul skimmed through *Strange Brother* and thought it looked more interesting than most of the titles. He moved further along and selected a thin volume with a green wrapper around it. He took the book from the shelf. At that moment Rolf came back into the room. Paul started guiltily and dropped the book onto the floor.

Rolf placed a brass tray, which held coffee cups and a long-handled copper pot of Turkish coffee, on a side table.

'I see you've been examining my books,' he said, walking over to Paul. He stooped to rescue the fallen volume from the floor.

'Ah!' he said. *'The Green Bay Tree.* A very curious play. I saw it when I was on holiday in London some years ago. Here,' he added, taking a programme from the front of the book and unfolding it. He handed the programme to Paul.

Paul looked down at the programme in his hand. He read the purple lettering.

'St Martin's Theatre.' He said the words out loud. '*The Green Bay Tree* by Mordaunt Shairp. Programme Fourpence.'

'You can read English?'

'*Ja.* I learned it at school.'

Paul handed the theatre programme back to Rolf.

'There was a very fine actor in the play. A man called Frank Vosper. He gave a most distinguished performance,' Rolf said folding the programme and slipping it back inside the covers of the book. He replaced the book on the shelf.

'And there was a young man called Hugh Williams who was almost as beautiful as you are.'

Rolf touched Paul's cheek softly and stared intently into his eyes.

'Don't be shy,' he said. 'You are a very beautiful boy.'

Paul blushed. He was embarrassed. Yet he felt a curious surge of pleasure at being complimented on his good looks.

'I've never done anything like this,' he whispered. His voice was hoarse and his heart pounded in his breast. He could feel a tremendous stirring between his legs. The room seemed to be suddenly charged with an electric tension which was almost palpable.

'Don't be afraid,' Rolf said. 'I won't force you to do

anything you don't want to do. I wouldn't hurt you. We are friends, remember?'

Paul could feel the shape of the mouth-organ through the fabric of his trousers. He touched it as if it were a talisman.

'Come. Let us have some coffee before it grows cold,' Rolf said. 'It is strong and sweet and good.'

Rolf led Paul over to one of the sofas. They sat down and while Rolf busied himself with pouring coffee Paul flipped through a pile of magazines on the table to one side of him.

'Some of them are rather old, I'm afraid,' Rolf said. 'I'm afraid I'm rather a jackdaw when it comes to collecting things.'

Paul tugged a small magazine from the pile. 'I see what you mean,' he said. 'This one is years old.'

Rolf took the magazine from Paul. '*Die Insel*,' he said. 'Yes. It ceased publication long ago. In its day it was a pioneering publication. But not the kind of thing that Nazis approve of at all.'

'But why not?' Paul asked.

'Look through it and you will see,' Rolf said, passing the magazine back to Paul.

On the cover was a photograph of a youth dressed in lederhosen who smiled out coyly at the camera. The picture seemed innocent enough to Paul. Slowly he turned the pages. The text looked heavy and boring but there were some pages of glossy photographs the first showed a heavily muscled young man standing naked by the side of a football. Paul began to understand. He turned the page. On the back of the photograph of the naked man was printed a list of books.

'*Bücher über Homosexualität*', Paul read. 'Books on homosexuality.'

He continued to turn the pages of the magazine. There were more pages of text, then two more photographs. One of the pictures showed another muscular youth; the second depicted a young boy standing between two trees in what was obviously a forest glade.

Paul closed the magazine.

'Did you find them attractive,' Rolf asked softly.

Paul shook his head. 'Not especially,' he said. 'Do you?'

Rolf took a sip from his cup of coffee. 'Not really,' he said. 'None of the boys in that magazine are really my type.'

For a moment there was silence. Paul became aware that the light outside was slowly fading from the sky. It must be getting quite late.

'What time is it?' he asked.

Rolf looked down at his wrist watch. 'It's getting on for eight o'clock,' he said.

'Perhaps I should be going.'

'Do you *really* want to go?' Rolf asked.

'No,' Paul said slowly. 'No. I don't think I do.'

'Good,' Rolf said happily. 'That settles that. Now, how about some more coffee?'

Paul nodded. Rolf refilled their cups.

'Can I ask you something?' Paul asked.

'Certainly.'

Paul paused and when he spoke he was nervous and hesitant. 'Are there many men ... are there many men who are like you?'

Rolf laughed. 'Heavens, yes,' he said. 'Thousands, probably, just here in Berlin. Men. And women, too.'

He became serious. 'But our way of life is dangerous now. The Nazis persecute us. Life was always difficult but now ... at times it seems impossible. They have closed the clubs and bars which once made Berlin a mecca for homosexuals from all over Europe. A few years ago there seemed to be a boy bar on every corner. The situation was very different then. All that has changed, been swept away by the Nazis and the people like them. Those they didn't arrest and imprison fled from Germany. They went to France or Holland, Switzerland, as far as America. Or to England – like the friend who gave me that piano.'

Rolf stopped speaking; he lifted his coffee cup and drained it. Carefully he replaced the small cup on the saucer.

'Things can be hard,' he murmured softly.

'But why do the Nazis not like men like you?' Paul asked.

For a moment Rolf reflected on Paul's question. 'It is not

only the Nazis,' he explained. 'It is not only men like me who are hated. People everywhere hate what is different, what they cannot understand. It doesn't matter if that difference is because you are homosexual or Jewish, gypsy or black, a writer or a painter, an actor or a drug addict. To be different is dangerous. People hate and fear what is different because it is outside their realm of comprehension. Men and women who are different from the mass of the population are viewed as an enemy; they are looked upon as deserters from the community at large. Those of us who are different, who wish to express ourselves as individuals, who wish to find our own way as opposed to the way set down by the rules of society, appear to be a threat against the order of *their* world.'

Rolf stood up. 'I mustn't be so serious,' he said. 'Would you like to hear some music?'

'If you like,' Paul answered.

Rolf walked across to the gramophone and selected a record. 'I hope you don't mind musical comedy,' he said. 'It's one of my passions.'

He cranked the machine and set the needle on the record. Music filled the room.

'This is from *Rose Marie*,' Rolf explained. 'I used to buy all the latest songs from the big American and English shows.'

'Have you ever been in a musical play?' Paul asked.

'I'm afraid not,' Rolf told him. 'My singing voice isn't up to it.'

'What films have you been in?' Paul enquired.

'Oh, lots. But funnily enough the film I am most proud of acting in wasn't something many people would have seen. I'm sure it's probably banned now – if it hasn't been destroyed.'

'What was that?'

'It was called *Gesetze der Liebe*,' Rolf said. '*The Laws of Love*. The film was made ten years ago, when things were very different in Germany.'

'What was it about?' Paul asked.

'What Doktor Hirschfeld used to call "the third sex",' Rolf explained. 'Men like me. It was when I was making the film that I first met Conrad. Conrad Veidt. He took the main role.'

The record stopped playing, and there was the sound of the scratching of the needle as it caught in the final groove.

Rolf walked across to the machine and lifted the arm from the record. He turned the record over and set the needle down again.

'Tell me some more about yourself, Paul,' Rolf said. 'I seem to have been doing all the talking.'

'There's not much to tell,' Paul said.

'Perhaps a drink will refresh your memory,' Rolf suggested. 'Would you like a glass of schnaps?'

'If it isn't too much trouble, I'd rather have something to eat,' Paul said.

'Will some bread and sausage do you?' Rolf asked. '*And* a glass of schnaps?'

Rolf placed the empty coffee cups on the tray and walked into the kitchen. Paul heard the click of plates and bottles and glasses.

'Here,' Rolf said, coming back into the room and placing the laden tray on the table. 'Help yourself.'

Paul carved thick slices of sausage and tore off a piece of bread. 'This is good,' he said.

'I don't know where you put it all,' Rolf chuckled.

Paul winked. 'As you say, I am a growing boy.'

The light had almost gone from the sky by now. The room was in semi-darkness. Paul stretched. He stood up and walked over to the window and peered down into the street. Rolf watched him intently.

'I feel much better now,' Paul said, turning back into the room to face Rolf. 'Perhaps a little tired.'

Paul stifled a yawn.

'Would you like to rest?' Rolf asked.

A small smile flickered across Paul's face. 'Yes,' he said. 'I think I would like that very much. And how about you? Do you also want to *rest*?'

Rolf remained silent for a moment, carefully studying the expression on Paul's face. He nodded slowly.

'If you will permit it, yes. I would like very much to *rest*,' Rolf answered.

Rolf stood up and led Paul through to the small, cramped bedroom. Most of the space in the room was taken up by a large double bed, covered by a down-filled quilt. A vast oak wardrobe stood at the foot of the bed and to either side of it were placed simple functional chairs. At either side of the head of the bed was a night table on which stood a lamp, ashtrays and books and scripts.

'Hang your clothes on that chair,' Rolf said, pointing to a chair on the far side of the bed.

Slowly Paul began to unbutton his shirt. Yet now he was nervous and self-conscious, aware of the older man across the room from him. Suddenly his fingers seemed to have grown insensitive and clumsy; he could hardly feel the buttons on his shirt. He removed the shirt and placed it neatly over the back of the chair Rolf had indicated. He tugged his vest off over his head. He gave a slight shiver as the cool night air caressed his body.

Covertly, Paul glanced at Rolf. He observed that the man had already taken off his shirt and vest and was now unbuttoning his trousers. He noted that Rolf's body was finely muscled and that the blue of his thick veins showed through the white of the skin of his arms. Paul felt a strange thrill of anticipation and guiltily turned away. He heard the rustle of fabric as Rolf removed his trousers; then the springs of the bed creaked as Rolf climbed between the sheets. For a moment Paul was completely still, like some shy forest animal frightened by the intrusion of man, poised as if for flight away from the unknown. Then he quickly took off his clothing. He turned to face Rolf.

'You are beautiful,' Rolf said very softly. 'Come.' He patted the bed.

'Do you mind if I turn out the light?' Paul asked.

Rolf shrugged. 'I don't mind. But I would love to be able to watch you.'

Paul gazed at Rolf. 'I'd feel better in the dark,' he said.

'Very well,' Rolf nodded.

Paul padded on his bare feet across the room, acutely aware that Rolf was observing every portion of his naked body. He heard Rolf give a deep sigh. Then he switched out the light. Now the room was illuminated only by the faint gleam of the moon and such light as shone into the room from the street outside. Paul moved toward the bed and climbed in beside Rolf.

Paul lay tensely, listening to the sound of his own heavy breathing and conscious of the fast pounding of his heart. The palms of his hands were damp with sweat and though he longed to move his legs he kept them rigidly clamped together. He knew that soon Rolf would touch him and he wondered what it would be like. He could feel himself rising to erection. He became aware that Rolf's left hand was reaching out towards him and that his body was turning and edging closer to him. As if without knowing it, Paul rolled on to his side and faced Rolf.

'*Liebling*,' Rolf whispered, and reached out his arms and pulled Paul close to him until their bodies were clasped tightly together.

'Darling,' Rolf repeated gently.

Paul could feel the excitement surging through his body as Rolf's hands began to move. Suddenly everything seemed right. This was what he wanted. His body responded hungrily to Rolf's touch.

'Yes, yes,' he murmured, as Rolf's cool, slim fingers closed around his erection.

*

As they lay in bed, side by side, in the light of the following morning, Paul felt an overwhelming sense of contentment. For what seemed like the first time in his life he was happy; it was as if the missing pieces of a complicated jigsaw puzzle had been found and slotted neatly into place. He rolled over and smiled up at Rolf.

'Are you happy?' Rolf asked.

Paul nodded.

'I am pleased,' Rolf said, smiling. 'For *I* am very, very happy.'

The early morning sounds from the street percolated up to them.

'The world is getting up,' Paul said. 'Perhaps I should be going.'

Rolf gazed at him. His face was suddenly serious. 'I have been thinking,' Rolf said.

Paul waited for Rolf to continue speaking, but for a moment it looked as if the man were completely lost in thought.

'I have been thinking, Paul,' Rolf repeated. 'Are you happy in the room in which you live?'

'It is all right,' Paul answered. 'But I do not especially *like* it.'

'I thought not,' Rolf said. 'Do you like it here?'

Paul nodded.

'And do you like me?'

Paul nodded again. He could feel the excitement bubbling inside him. He suspected he knew where Rolf's questioning would lead.

'Would you be happy here, do you think?'

'Oh, yes. I would be *very* happy here,' Paul answered.

'It is a long time since I met anyone like you,' Rolf said. 'It is a long time since I met anyone I wanted to be with as much as I already know I want to be with you. I know that the idea of love at first sight is probably silly and romantic and completely unlikely. Yet I also know that I think I fell in love with you the instant I saw you in the Tiergarten yesterday afternoon. Do you understand me?'

'Yes. I think so,' Paul answered.

'That is good,' Rolf said. 'Well, Paul. What I'm trying to say is this: Would you like to move into this little flat with me?'

'Would I?' Paul grinned. 'You bet!'

*

At first, life for Paul and Rolf proceeded smoothly. As the days and weeks passed, they grew closer together and established a firm bond of love and trust. Initially, Paul had been slightly doubtful about moving in with Rolf; he had wondered how long the relationship could last before Rolf tired of him and threw him out onto the streets of Berlin to fend for himself. Gradually, however, he grew to appreciate that Rolf loved him and that he would not do anything to harm him. The passion Rolf felt for Paul was fully reciprocated and when the two of them were together, Paul was completely secure and comfortable.

Early in the morning, when he had work, Rolf would go off to the film studios to act a part (although he complained that most of the films in production in Germany were no better than National Socialist propaganda for Doktor Goebbels, he needed the fees he was paid as he did not wish to live on the money he had saved). While Rolf was at the studios, Paul would potter around the apartment – clearing away the cups and dishes from their evening meal, tidying the rooms, browsing through books and magazines. When the weather was fine, Paul would explore Berlin or spend hours gazing at the animals in the Zoological Gardens to which he would travel in the elevated railway. Rolf gave Paul a small allowance, for though Paul desperately wanted to work he still could not find a job of any kind. The days passed quickly; there was no time for boredom now, for Paul was experiencing a way of life which was completely different from that which he had known in Riesbach. Each new day brought some new experience and, however small it might be, or however simple, it gave Paul pleasure. And what gave Paul pleasure made Rolf happy.

In the evenings, when Rolf had returned from the studios, they would have dinner and then go for walks about Berlin. On these walks each would tell stories about his past life; Paul talking about Riesbach, his father and mother, the Hitler Youth (of which he had been an unwilling member); Rolf speaking of his family, about his Polish grandfather who had been a clown in the circus and who had travelled all over Europe, performing before the Kaiser and, in England, before King Edward VII. Rolf's family seemed to be very glamorous to Paul, far removed from his own mother and father whose lives seemed positively humdrum in comparison. But circus life wasn't all excitement, Rolf told Paul and explained that most of it had been spent on the move. It hadn't been until his grandfather retired that he had settled down in Germany, in Frankfurt where Rolf had been born and where he had grown up.

Sometimes everything seemed to be going too well and Paul would feel a shiver of apprehension at what might happen in the future. Then two events occurred which prompted Rolf to suggest they leave Berlin.

One evening, as they were coming out of a cinema, two elderly women recognised Rolf.

'Isn't that Rolf Hagen?' one of the women had said, nudging her friend and gesturing in the direction of Rolf and Paul.

The second woman had stared hard for a moment and then nodded. 'Yes, I believe it is,' she had said. 'And by the look of that boy he is with I'd think he ought to be more careful.'

The woman had nodded meaningfully. 'I don't think *that* kind of thing should be flaunted,' she had continued. 'It's downright disgusting – not to mention criminal.'

The two women had moved briskly away, sniffing pointedly as they passed Rolf and Paul.

The incident was unpleasant, and instead of going to a bar as they usually did after seeing a film, Paul and Rolf returned immediately to the apartment. Rolf was shaken, though with the innocence of his youth Paul was hardly aware of what had happened.

The second disturbing event occurred only a short time after the first, and the two taken together had a distinctly cumulative effect on Paul and Rolf. It had been a crisp, bright November Sunday; they had been promenading in the Tiergarten, enjoying the weak winter sunshine. They had been walking slowly along the Sieges-Allee, Rolf making amusing comments about the marble statues of the Prussian rulers which flanked their route. Suddenly Paul had stopped walking, a nervous expression on his face.

'What is wrong, Paulie?' Rolf had asked.

'There's someone from Riesbach coming this way,' Paul had explained.

'What harm can that do?' Rolf asked.

'It's Franz Mantner,' Paul told him. 'He is a great friend of my father; they joined the Party together.'

Rolf had stared ahead and noticed a group of three men strolling casually towards them.

'Shall we turn back?' he asked. 'We can pretend you have not seen them.'

Paul shook his head. 'No,' he said. 'It's no good pretending. Let's go on.'

As the three men drew level with Paul and Rolf one of them stepped forward.

'Hullo, Paul,' he said. '*Wie gehts*? All of them in Riesbach have been wondering where you'd gone and what you were up to. Now they'll know.'

Mantner had given a suggestive snigger.

'Good afternoon, Herr Mantner,' Paul had said, his voice cracking with nervousness.

'Yes,' Mantner had continued, 'I can see you've done all right for yourself.'

Mantner had winked at Paul.

'I d-don't know what you mean,' Paul stuttered.

Mantner gave a coarse laugh. 'You don't have to pretend with me, Paul,' he said. 'I've got the picture sure enough.'

Paul blushed.

'Well, we must be going,' Mantner said. 'Goodbye, Paul. I will be sure to give your best regards to your papa.'

The three men had moved off along the path. The sound of laughter drifted back towards Paul and Rolf.

'Come,' Rolf said, gently patting Paul on the shoulder. 'Let us go home.'

Once back at the apartment, Paul had confessed his fear that his father would travel to Berlin to find him and force him to return to Riesbach.

'I would rather die than return there,' he had protested.

Rolf had made coffee and, as they sipped from their cups, had proposed a plan.

'It is obvious that things in Berlin are not safe for either of us,' he said. 'We must get away. But I don't think we can be secure anywhere in Germany. We must leave the country.'

'But where can we go?' Paul asked.

Rolf was silent for a moment. 'To England, I think,' Rolf said. 'I have many friends there who would help us. Conrad Veidt is working there. Alex Korda is a big man in British films. I was great friends with him when he was trying to make a go of things here in Berlin years ago. I am sure that either Conrad or Alex would help me to find work in the films in England.'

'I do not have papers though,' Paul told Rolf.

'I know, I know. Do not worry. If you know the right people and if you have a little money ... it is possible to get a passport and exit papers. I am sure that travel documents can be produced for you.'

In the days which followed, Rolf made his preparations for their departure from Berlin. He wrote many letters to friends, especially to those who had settled in England. He kept mysterious assignations which were not without danger in connection with obtaining travel documents for Paul. He discreetly let it be known that he wished to dispose of the lease of the apartment and that he was willing to sell most of the furnishings. He escorted Paul to a photographer to obtain photographs for his passport. Slowly the preparations came close to fruition.

An acquaintance from the British Embassy who admired Rolf as an actor and understood the problems that Rolf *the man* faced introduced an English woman who admired Hitler with a passion which – to Rolf – was bordering on the hysterical. The woman disliked Rolf on sight; Rolf loathed her. But the apartment was exactly what she was looking for. She purchased the lease and most of the contents of the flat – the books and pictures and personal objects were to be stored by a friend of Rolf's and, happily, she paid with a cheque which could be drawn on her London bank account.

From friends in London letters arrived in which offers of

assistance and pledges of support were made. More important, Korda had written to Rolf promising him a small part in a film called *Dark Journey* which had a script by Lajos Biro, an old friend, and which was to star another friend, Conrad Veidt.

As each element of the plan fitted neatly together, and as the day of their departure drew nearer, Rolf and Paul found that they were becoming nervous. Each time they heard footsteps on the stairs, they suspected it could be the Gestapo come to arrest them. Each day they became more tense, unable to believe that their luck could hold and that they would be permitted to leave Berlin without problems.

Finally the day of their departure arrived. The books had been taken from the shelves and packed in boxes; the pictures had been carefully wrapped in sacking; everything that had not been sold and that was to remain in Berlin had been despatched to the friend who was to keep it in store.

Rolf and Paul stood in the middle of the main room, staring around at the empty bookshelves and the spaces on the walls where the pictures had once hung.

'We are setting out on a dangerous journey,' Rolf told Paul. 'I have taken every possible precaution to make sure that nothing goes wrong. But these are insane times. Anything could happen.'

Paul nodded.

'I must ask you this question one last time,' Rolf continued. 'Are you absolutely certain you wish to come with me? Are you sure you wish to face the uncertainty of exile?'

Paul did not pause for even an instant of thought. 'Yes,' he said softly. 'I am quite certain. I want to be with you.'

Rolf smiled. 'Good,' he said. 'Now I think it is time for us to leave.'

For the last time, they had looked around at the flat. Both felt a sense of sadness at leaving, yet the sorrow was mingled with a feeling of excitement caused by the thought of a new life opening up for them.

'One last thing,' Rolf said as they moved towards the door

of the apartment. 'If anyone should ask you, remember to tell them that you are my nephew and that you are coming for a holiday in London while I am making a film.'

Paul nodded. Rolf opened the door and they picked up their bags and began to walk slowly down the stairs.

*

The journey had gone smoothly. The German officials had hardly taken any notice of Rolf and Paul when they crossed the frontier into Holland. Ironically, the first hint of trouble had appeared when they landed from the ferry at Harwich. The British customs officials had not been particularly friendly, perhaps suspecting that Rolf and Paul were refugees without proper papers or any means of support. Rolf knew that people had been turned back, placed back on the ferry and returned to Europe. However, the letter from Korda promising work, the cheque from the fanatical English woman, the cash which Rolf carried with him, and the letter from a small London hotel announcing that rooms had been reserved for them, eventually convinced the officials. Once Rolf and Paul had filled out the appropriate forms, detailing their names, addresses, the name and address of the hotel at which they would be staying, their passports were stamped and they were allowed to proceed with their journey to London.

The contrast between London and Berlin had been as overwhelming for Paul as had the contrast between Berlin and Riesbach. At first he found himself missing the sense of military bustle of Berlin and the great red flags with the white circle enclosing the swastika which had hung from so many buildings. But once he had become used to London he found he could enjoy a real sense of freedom from fear. He knew, too, that Rolf no longer had the fear that they might be seen together by some person who would denounce them.

Though the hotel they stayed in at first was inexpensive, Rolf decided they should find a small flat; some place which they could make into a proper home. In the days during which

Rolf was rehearsing for his film role, Paul would wander around the area to the north of the West End of London looking at flats which he had seen advertised on the noticeboards outside the local shops. Eventually a perfect little flat was found and rented.

The flat was located in Charlotte Street – a neighbourhood both bohemian and cosmopolitan. The flat was at the top of a building, the ground and first floors of which were occupied by a German restaurant. The rich smells of food which percolated up the winding stairs reminded Rolf and Paul of home, and often in the evening, when Rolf had returned from a day of filming, they would slip down the stairs to eat a meal in the restaurant.

Once he had become used to the sprawling size of London, Paul behaved exactly as would any young man loose on his own for the first time in a foreign city. He enjoyed walking and would spend hours wandering around the streets of London looking at the famous buildings: he waited outside Buckingham Palace and watched the changing of the guard; he visited the many museums and galleries; he walked down to the City and felt the pervading sense of history which emanated from every stone of the Tower of London; he was awed by the majesty and calm of St Paul's Cathedral; occasionally he would visit a pub.

Often, however, when the initial excitement of sightseeing had dissipated somewhat, Paul would spend his time talking to the staff of the German restaurant below. He would sit in a corner of the steamy kitchen, talking about life in Germany with the waiters and the kitchen staff. Soon he became so much a part of the family atmosphere which prevailed in the kitchen that he found himself helping with the more menial tasks. Eventually, the fat German widow who ran the place suggested that Paul might like to work for her – unofficially, of course, as he had no work permit. Paul was overjoyed at this offer of work (though a little saddened to consider that it was easier for him to find work in a foreign country than it had been at home in Germany). Now he was able to contribute money for living expenses, Paul felt he had become an adult.

Sometimes, after work, there were parties in the restaurant. Frau Mahler would sit at a table at the back of the main room and watch as her staff – and their friends and relations – ate, and drank vast quantities of beer and wine and tried to recreate the atmosphere of home. She had grown fond of Paul, treating him like a son, and she liked Rolf who was always invited down to the restaurant for the gatherings.

Less frequently, Rolf was invited to parties by actors or actresses he had either known in Germany or whom he had met since he had been in England. Naturally, Rolf would take Paul along to these parties. Yet somehow Paul didn't feel comfortable. Though he knew that it was not intended, Paul always felt as if he were simply tolerated because he was Rolf's friend. He had nothing in common with the glamorous men and women who sipped champagne and called each other 'Darling!' in laughing voices. He also became rather withdrawn and suspicious if anyone showed an exaggerated friendliness, and on one occasion he was acutely disturbed to realise that the young actor who had been helping him to food and drink was trying to persuade him to go home with him. Gently Paul had reminded the young man that he was with Rolf and that he would be going home with Rolf. He had walked away from the actor feeling, in some curious way, a sense of hurt. He had moved across the crowded room until he found Rolf. As Rolf sensed Paul's nearness he had turned and smiled warmly. Once again, Paul felt happy and secure.

Yet while life for Paul and Rolf moved calmly forward – working, living simply, happy in each other's company and with that of other refugees from Hitler's regime in Germany, the world whirled closer to the abyss of war. Confrontation seemed imminent; heedlessly life went on.

Then German Consulates all over the world were told to make Germans of fighting age return to the Fatherland. One morning official-looking letters arrived for Paul and Rolf. When they opened them, it was to discover that they contained orders to return to Germany.

'Surely I don't have to take any notice of it?' Paul said to Rolf.

'I wish you didn't,' Rolf said. 'I wish there was something we could do.'

'There must be,' Paul said. 'There has to be something.'

'I don't think so,' Rolf said. 'It is different for me. I have a work permit. But you have no permit and you can be arrested and imprisoned and then deported back to Germany as an illegal immigrant. Worse, if you refuse to go back now, the Embassy could make a fuss to ensure that you are deported. Then, I fear, things could be even worse for you in Germany. You would probably be sent to a prison camp before you were made to join the army.'

Paul could feel the hot tears in his eyes and angrily brushed them away with the back of his hand.

'What am I to do?' he asked.

Rolf looked immensely sad. 'I am afraid that you must go back. I can think of no way of escape.'

'But I don't want to go back,' Paul had cried, tears now streaming unashamedly down his face. 'I don't want to leave you. I want to be with you. Always.'

'*Liebling*,' Rolf said, wrapping his arms around Paul and rocking him gently to calm him. 'I don't want to be parted from you. But I cannot think of anything we can do. If there is to be a war, there is every chance that both of us would be interned here as enemy aliens. As I am moderately well-known, things are not so difficult for me. But how could I explain you? The English laws are no more gentle to our kind than those of Germany. If it were known that we had a relationship, we would be thrown out of this country. We are exiles from our own country and we are exiles from what most people accept as normal. Wherever we go, we could be treated as criminals.'

Paul stopped weeping. He extricated himself from Rolf's arms. He dried his eyes. Now he became calm. He nodded his head and smiled weakly at Rolf.

'I understand,' he said. 'I must face my responsibilities. I must return to Germany.'

Suddenly a small moan escaped from Rolf's lips.

'Oh, God,' he said. 'I want us to be together. I do not want this awful war which is surely going to happen. I love you. I love you very much. I cannot bear the thought of your being dragged away from me. Even worse, I cannot bear the thought that you can be taken from me and forced to fight and maybe die. You must live, we must be together again when the world has regained its sanity.'

*

With great sadness, Paul made his solitary way back across Europe to Germany. At first, he returned to Riesbach but it was obvious that Franz Mantner had talked to his father.

'You are no better than a whore,' Hermann Seidler had screamed at him, his face scarlet with rage. 'Get out of this house and never return. You are no son of mine. I will have nothing to do with you.'

Paul's mother had stood silently weeping. Paul had gazed helplessly at her.

'Your behaviour is a disgrace. Don't think I don't know what's been going on. You are lucky I don't report you for disgusting degenerate behaviour. Now go. I never want to see you again,' his father had shouted, spittle from his mouth hitting Paul in the face.

He had left the house, thinking that he would probably have no further contact with his parents. He was sad for his mother's sake; but perhaps it was best this way. He could cause her no more hurt now.

Paul reported to the military authorities. He was put into a tank regiment in training. The barracks were outside Frankfurt. He was far away from Riesbach – and even further away from London. He felt isolated and alone. After a few months, Paul's gloom began to dissipate. He began to enjoy life in the army, the beer-drinking with his comrades, the training which made his body trim and fit. The pain receded.

Yet each time he received a letter from Rolf from London, the wound would smart again. Memories would flood back and for a few days life became depressing. As letters could be censored, Rolf wrote to Paul care of a small bar he knew in

Frankfurt which was near to the camp where Paul was stationed. Rolf wrote every week and though the letters were extremely discreet, they were full of love and concern. One of the main themes of these letters was Rolf's desire to return to Germany and see Paul again before war broke out.

'Please, Rolf, do not come back,' Paul wrote. 'It is not safe. I love you and I shall always be grateful to you for all your kindness to me. But please do not come. It is too dangerous. When all this is over, we can be together again.'

One evening Paul walked into Frankfurt and entered the bar. He was longing for a beer and hoped that there would be a letter from Rolf waiting for him. He was a little worried. He had not heard from Rolf in nearly two weeks and had been visiting the bar whenever possible to see if a letter had yet arrived.

As he walked into the bar, quiet in the early evening, the owner had nodded a greeting at him.

'Are there any letters for me?' Paul asked.

The owner of the bar shook his head. 'No,' he said. Then he grinned and pointed to a dim corner of the bar. 'There's something better than a letter. There is a friend to see you.'

Paul stared across the room. As his eyes became accustomed to the gloom of the bar, he perceived a familiar figure sitting hunched up at a small table in the corner.

'Rolf,' he whispered to himself, as he hurried across to the seated figure.

'Rolf!' he said, seating himself across from his friend. 'Rolf, didn't you get my letter telling you it would be too dangerous for you to come back to Germany?'

'Paulie, Paulie,' Rolf said, beaming with pleasure. 'Of course I received your letter. But you should not worry on my account. I will be quite safe ... and I had to see you at least one more time.'

'If I had only known you were going to be here,' Paul said, 'I could have arrived earlier.'

'I had no way of contacting you at the camp,' Rolf explained. 'I thought it would be unsafe for both of us. I just had to pray that you would come in tonight.'

'I have so little time,' Paul said. 'I have to be back in camp by eleven. It is nine now. But it doesn't matter. I will stay with you.'

Rolf shook his head. 'No, *Liebling*. No. It would be foolish. They would put you on a charge if you stayed away from the camp all night. I do not wish to be the reason for getting you into any trouble.'

'Where are you staying?' Paul asked.

Rolf smiled at him. 'Not far. Not far, at all.'

'Where?'

'The landlord of this admirable inn has let me have one of his rooms.'

For a moment they gazed at each other in silence.

'I have an hour,' Paul said softly.

'Might I then invite you to see my room?' Rolf asked, as if he already knew what answer Paul would give.

Paul pushed his chair back from the table and stood up. 'After you,' he said.

Rolf stood up and moved towards the staircase at the side of the room. Following him, Paul began to climb the stairs. For an hour they were together again, and Paul couldn't believe that it was possible to love anyone quite so much.

7

The moon was high in the sky, and the sand of the desert glittered in the cold silver light. The air was tinged with a slight chill. Ken shivered. Paul stood facing him; there were tears in his eyes. He touched the thin silver chain around his neck.

'When we said goodbye,' Paul said, 'Rolf gave me this as a parting present.'

Paul unclasped the chain from around his neck and passed it across to Ken who avoided his gaze so as not to see the tears in his eyes.

'I was back in the camp by eleven,' Paul continued. 'And the next morning – so I was told later – Rolf left for England, taking the train to Paris ... But at the frontier they caught him.'

Paul was silent. Ken gazed at him without comprehension.

'Caught him?' Ken asked.

Paul nodded his head and swallowed hard.

'I don't understand ...' Ken said. 'Because he was a homosexual?'

Paul shook his head and looked up at Ken.

'Not only had Rolf been a well-known actor,' he said, 'he was known as a homosexual ... And he had Jewish blood.'

'Had ...?' Ken asked, staring steadily at Paul.

'He died. In a ... camp,' Paul said softly.

Ken looked away. There was silence for a moment.

'Poor Rolf ...' Ken said.

Ken found a packet of cigarettes and held it towards Paul. He offered him a light. Paul smoked his cigarette for a moment without speaking.

'*Danke*. Now do you understand?' Paul said, his voice hoarse with emotion.

Ken nodded. 'After what you've just told me, for Christ's sake, why do you fight for your Fatherland?' he asked.

'I get your meaning,' Paul said. 'But can I put a question to you?'

'Surely.'

'Do you know why *you* fight?'

'More or less,' Ken answered.

'Why?'

'Because I like England, I suppose.'

'In spite of slums and poverty?'

'Yes.'

'And I fight for Germany in spite of many *shrecklich* things that are done there. *Verstehen Sie?*'

'This Sergeant?'

'Mantner ... I know what you think. I had done it once – why not a second time?'

'Yes,' Ken said, nodding his head.

Paul's voice became firmer. 'It was completely different,' he said. 'Rolf was gentle. He was my friend ...'

'Couldn't Mantner be your friend?'

'Never!' Paul answered.

'Why not?'

'If you met him, you would know ... He is a pig ... In the punishment cells back in Frankfurt – there was a boy who fought against him when he tried it. But Mantner had a club. And the man who was in the cell next door could hear the boy screaming. By morning the boy was dead.'

'We've got bastards like that in the glass-houses back home – don't worry,' Ken said. ' "In the morning the prisoner was found hung in his cell." You bet he was. Hung so he couldn't tell what they'd done to him. Anyhow, we're away from the lot of them now.'

'*Gott sei Dank*.'

'Never let the bastards get you down. That's my creed in life,' Ken said.

He stood up and walked over to Paul and punched him affectionately.

Paul grinned. 'Perhaps, after all, you're stronger than I am,' he said.

'I doubt it.'

Ken moved away from Paul, towards the battered canvas chair. He rested a foot against one of the struts of the chair and stared across at Paul.

'Pity the tank wireless is broken,' Ken said. 'If it was working we could call up a Sergeant or two. "Hullo Mantner ... Hullo Mantner. Preston calling. Over." "Allo Preston ... *Hier ist* Mantner answerink ... Ofer ..." "Hullo Mantner, Preston calling ... Message from General Rommel reads ... Dig a deep trench latrine twenty feet wide and ten feet deep ... Over." "Allo Preston, Mantner answerink ... Orders received and understood and obeyed. Vot next? Ofer." "Now take a running jump and drown yourself in it. Over." '

Ken sat down angrily on the chair.

'And I might send greetings to our RSM and that old bastard Captain Baldock,' he said fiercely.

It suddenly seemed much darker. Ken looked up. Clouds had obscured the moon. The only light now came from the two oil-lamps.

Paul gazed towards Ken. 'It's not possible – but if it were,' he said, 'if it were possible to clear right out of it, would you go?'

'I've been wondering that for the last three days ... I'm not sure. Would you?'

'Under certain conditions – yes.'

Ken leaned forward in the chair. 'I'd need more time to think it over,' he said after a moment of deep thought.

'That convoy I was expecting to come south was due three days ago,' Paul told him. 'It's certainly been called off.'

'Or it passed beyond the horizon,' Ken said.

Paul nodded. 'So we may have another week – at the rate the food is lasting out,' he said.

Ken and Paul gazed at each other without speaking. Paul brushed a strand of hair away from his forehead.

'Tell me something,' he said. 'Have you a brother or sister?'

'An elder sister. She's married to a dentist in Uckfield. So if he knocks her teeth out, he can always put them back again,' Ken said, grinning.

'I was an only child.'

'So I gathered.'

Paul stood up. He thrust his hands into the pockets of his shorts.

'When you are alone,' he said, 'do you make up stories for yourself?'

'Dozens.'

Paul smiled. 'I can imagine,' he said. 'Do you know, Ken, I've never had a girlfriend?'

'You must have done.'

'No,' Paul replied. 'Because at home I was seldom allowed out. I have never had a girl.'

'What about the luscious great beauty in Naples? The one you showed me the snap of?' Ken asked.

'As you said, she was not a girl. She was a tart. A painted lady. A whore of Babylon.'

'With great big ...'

'Tits.'

'Well, anyhow, you went to bed with a woman,' Ken said.

'*Bestimmt*. Yes. It began just like the story I used to tell myself ... I picked up the woman in a bar. I went back to her room. I went to bed with her. I "had it" with her ... But then it all changed ... After it was over ... She got out of bed and started to dress ... She insisted that I too get up ... She demanded her payment and I paid it. There was nothing romantic about it to her. It was just a cheap commercial transaction ... There were other men waiting on the stairs outside. *Verstehen Sie?*'

Ken laughed. 'Only too well,' he said. 'Last time we got back to Alex, I was a gibbering sex maniac. "A bint" I cried to the taxi driver. And he promptly drove me to a Military Brothel. Well, I didn't much like the idea of doing it to

attention, but I entered a room numbered with a great "E".
No trace of a bint. But a bloody great tube of ointment on the
table – and above it a huge printed instruction: "Apply
ointment according to directions". So I did. And it was pure
anguish; tears of pain poured down my cheeks. And so on to
room "F". And there, lying in a splendid bed – army issue –
was a lovely bint, looking up at me, all expectant. "Why-for
you cry?" the bint asked me. "Because they've wrecked me," I
said. "They've unmanned me – probably for good." And I
gave her a hundred piastres and a chaste kiss on the forehead.
And clutching myself, I staggered out into the street.'

Paul laughed. Ken grinned at him.

'Not bloody funny, mate,' Ken said. 'I can tell you.'

'But my trouble was different,' Paul began. 'I'd thought of it
in my mind as so different. Then I knew that the story I had
told myself over the years could never come true – because in
my story the girl and I had made love all night and in the
morning we still wanted each other.'

'It will happen to you – one day,' Ken reassured him.

'Never!' Paul said.

'You can't tell ...'

'I can,' Paul replied. 'I can tell, from today ...'

Ken shook his head.

'Do you remember you laughed when I told you that I was
expecting a visitor?' Paul asked. 'Well ... in my story, so I
was.'

Ken laughed again. 'In your story, I suppose you expected a
young Bedouin girl to come wandering across the desert?'

Ken was smiling, but Paul's face was solemn once again.
'No,' Paul said. 'Nor a girl from the Italian brothel. I was
expecting a soldier ... of my own age. In my story – *natürlich* –
he was of my own age, and he was German.'

Ken was watching Paul's face in silence, but Paul would not
meet his gaze. He was staring at the sand at his feet.

'In my story,' Paul continued, 'the soldier is lost and he has
been wounded a little in the arm, and he has run out of food
and water. So – *natürlich* – he is very glad to see me. And I
bandage his arm and I give him plenty to eat and to drink. *Er*

ist sehr nett, sehr sympatisch ... And during the day we become friends. So we talk about nearly everything. We have supper ... We talk a little more ... And then we fall silent ... And at that moment each of us is probably thinking that we are very much alone together – with no one else around for many miles. In my story, we have only one lamp alight. But we decide that we must leave it alight all night – as *we* have done each night, so that a passing convoy or patrol, seeing the light, will come towards it.'

For an instant, Paul looked towards his bivouac.

'I have made him a bed of blankets in a corner beneath the tarpaulin,' Paul continued. 'And presently we undress and get into our beds ... And I lie there, wondering ... I can feel my heart thumping ... Suddenly he stretches over to the lamp, which is beside him in my story, and turns it down. This is all in my story, of course.'

Paul lowered his head. His hands were clenched tightly together.

''Then he leans over and blows out the flame, so that we are in darkness,' Paul said, speaking as if to himself. 'And then I know ... I know what he feels ... And in my story, he comes over to me ...'

For a moment there was complete silence. Paul and Ken sat completely still, listening to the soft noises of the desert around them.

'So that's it,' Ken said, speaking very quietly.

'Yes,' Paul answered. 'But it is only a story I told myself when I was alone here.'

'I understand.'

'I don't think so ... I wish you did.'

'I'm not an idiot, as you called me.'

'Then do you understand why I can now tell you the story?'

'No,' Ken replied.

'I can now tell you – because it was only in my mind. Life has wiped away the dream ... *Und warum?* ... Because – for the first time – life has been kinder and truer. For the first time, life has been better.'

Ken turned slowly away from Paul and kicked at the track lying broken on the sand.

'Do you understand me?' Paul asked.

Ken nodded his head.

'Are you angry?' Paul asked. 'Have I offended you?'

After a brief pause, Ken shook his head.

'But you don't ...'

'Look,' Ken blurted out suddenly, 'you and me ... we're on different tracks ...'

'Do you despise me?'

'Of course not.'

Ken hesitated, then turned and looked directly at Paul. Their eyes met.

'Don't worry,' Ken said gently. 'You'll be all right, Paul. You'll find someone.'

'I don't want to find someone,' Paul cried out. 'Since I've lost Rolf, I didn't know who the person would be ... But I knew that I could tell.'

'I'm on a different track,' Ken said softly. 'That's the problem. I told you. It's no good.'

'I would have said that once,' Paul cried out violently, moving away from the tank and beginning to walk towards the open desert.

'Where are you going?' Ken asked quietly.

Paul stopped walking. 'I'm not leaving ... I'm all right,' he said. 'I just want to be away from the tank for a while.'

'And away from me?' Ken asked softly.

Paul started to walk again. Ken stood up and moved after Paul, out into the dark, shifting sand of the desert. Ken remained a few paces behind Paul, who neither looked back or to either side of him. He seemed to be plunging blindly into the sand – as if it were waves which could catch hold of him and tow him far away from this solitary spot. Now the shell of the tank was almost out of sight, hidden behind a dune.

Abruptly, Paul stopped walking and Ken almost collided with him. Paul stood silently staring out into the desert, as if somewhere out there in the dark night he might find an answer to his problems. His arms hung slackly by his sides. For a few minutes Ken watched Paul's back, the slightly hunched shoulders, the whole way he stood which suggested deep despair. Instinctively, Ken moved closer to Paul and clasped him in a tight embrace.

Paul stared into Ken's eyes, but his arms continued to hang limply at his sides.

'*Danke,*' Paul said. 'You are kind, and I am grateful for your sympathy. And perhaps one day you could feel real love for me. I can only hope. But I understand what you feel.'

Paul gently disengaged himself from Ken's arms and turned to walk slowly back towards the shell of the tank.

8

The sun's rays slanting across the desert like gently probing
fingers awoke Ken early the next morning. It was only in the
first light of morning or in the last glorious moments of the
days as the sun started to sink below the horizon that the
desert was at all tolerable. For most of the daylight hours the
heat was unbearable; for most of the hours of the night the
temperature changed completely, becoming surprisingly cold.

Ken snuggled into his blankets for a few moments of
contemplation; he was relaxed and enjoyed a sense of physical
well-being. Gradually he shrugged himself free of his bedding
and sat up and gazed around him. As he peered around him,
the sun rose slowly higher in the sky and caused the deep
shadows on the sand to shorten. Ken stood up and stretched.
With a wonderful sense of laziness he scratched the coarse
hair at the base of his stomach. He stared across the narrow
patch of sand towards Paul's bivouac. Paul was lying in a
foetal position in the sleeping bag, still deeply asleep.

Ken tugged on his shorts and put on his bush shirt. He then
picked up a tin of water and moved a little way from the tank
to perform his morning ablutions. Once he had relieved
himself and had a wash, Ken decided to make further
investigations of the tank. He heaved himself up onto the body
of the machine and bent over the edge of the reeking turret. He
shuddered as he looked at the evidence of carnage down there,
but then he leaned forward and stretched his arm inside. He
hauled up various relics of battle which were no better than
motes of dust in the eye of God. Then his hand gripped a

leather strap and he hauled up a battered haversack. Some instinct made him take it out of the tank and away from the view of the still sleeping German.

The straps on the haversack were already half open. Pulling the buckles free, Ken peered inside. He pulled out two rusting spanners, a torch which no longer worked (the batteries were obviously flat), a chipped tin mug, and a small square canvas box. Ken recognised the shape of the box immediately for it was the container for a compass. He was trembling as he lifted the flap and peered inside. The compass was intact; it didn't appear to be damaged in any way. He took the compass from the canvas box and moved further away from the tank because he knew that the metal would affect the magnetic needle of the compass.

The sun was well above the horizon as Ken pointed the compass toward it and looked through the prism. The needle swung round rapidly for a moment and then the movements slowed until the needle became completely still: it pointed a few degrees away from North. Ken experimented with the compass several times and – to his intense excitement – realised that it was in perfect working order.

They were saved! Already a plan began to form in Ken's mind. Gleefully, he hurried across to Paul's bivouac.

'Wakee, wakee,' he called out cheerfully.

Paul did not stir.

'Rise and shine,' Ken shouted. 'Get up you lazy, idle Kraut.'

Ken raised a clenched fist to his lips and imitated a bugle call; then he impersonated 'The Last Post'. He gave a playful kick to Paul's body in the sleeping bag. Paul opened his eyes and stared blankly up at Ken.

'Rise and shine, rise and shine,' Ken shouted, jumping around in his excitement.

'Hello,' Paul said sleepily. 'You seem very lively this morning.'

'I shall report you to Erwin,' Ken said smiling, as Paul pulled himself free of the sleeping bag and tugged on his shorts.

'Why is that?' Paul asked.

'You said the compass was broken.'

'I did.'

'It's not broken. It's not broken at all. You crafty fucking Kraut.'

'I thought it was broken,' Paul protested.

'Are you listening to me?' Ken demanded.

'Yes, I am listening.'

'Do you realise what I am saying?'

Paul shook his head. 'I do not feel properly awake yet, Ken,' he said sleepily.

'We have a compass!'

'Does that make any difference?'

Ken gave a mocking laugh. 'Does that make any difference, the boy asks. Course it fucking does, you stupid great Kraut.'

'What difference?'

'I just don't believe it,' Ken said with a grin. 'Well, old son, it means we can leave here for a start.'

'And go where?' Paul asked.

'I don't know about you, but *I've* made up *my* mind,' Ken said. 'I'm sick of this fucking war. I'm off.'

'You can't just off,' Paul told him, shuffling lazily forward to the primus stove and lighting it.

'While you were snoring away these last few minutes, I've been thinking things over. Now then, if one is going to plan, one must plan logically, as Mr Carey our poor benighted troop leader kept telling us ... so what are the alternatives?'

'What?' Paul asked, placing a can of water on top of the primus.

'Well,' Ken began, 'we could always stay here and die of thirst. That's a plan. Or you could march off smartly to the west, and I could stride away bravely to the east. That's another plan.'

'Who carries the compass?' Paul enquired.

'I do, of course,' Ken replied. 'You said it was broken. Alternatively we could both move south. Do you know about the Senussi Bedouin down south?'

'*Bestimmt*,' Paul said, nodding his head. 'They are killers.'

'It depends which side you're on,' Ken told him. 'If we're taken prisoner by your lot and escape we're told to head south to the Senussi black tents, because they've got a soft spot for the British. So we pack up as much food and water as we can carry and we move south for the Senussi.'

'But what about me?' Paul asked. 'Would they help a German?'

'But you wouldn't be a German,' Ken told him. 'You'd be a gunner from the Crusader tank I was in. If a single Senussi speaks a word of English, which I doubt, he's hardly likely to spot your accent, is he?'

'Maybe not,' Paul answered.

'Another thing, the Senussi are all related, and they're strung out right across the Sahara. Give one Senussi an old cap badge and you've bought yourself a passage right through to South Africa. *Fabelhaft?*'

'*Fabelhaft,*' Paul agreed cautiously. 'But what then?'

'Some of the Afrikaaners are on the Jerries' side, aren't they?' Ken asked.

'Well, some for sure,' Paul answered. 'We are told that if we are sent to one of your prison camps in South Africa there may be Afrikaaners who will try to help us.'

'So you'd be all right if you could find an Afrikaaners farm,' Ken suggested. 'You'd tell them you are an escaped prisoner. So you'd be laughing.'

'But what about you?' Paul asked gently.

For an instant Ken hesitated, then he smiled across at Paul.

'I'm a good swimmer,' he said, and laughed.

'Oh, Ken. Do be serious for once,' Paul protested.

Ken gave a good-natured grimace.

'Couldn't you work on the farm also?' Paul asked.

'I'd have to see, wouldn't I?'

'Listen, Ken ...' Paul began. 'Last night, it was a mistake to tell you my dream. But people ... people do sometimes say things.'

'Forget it, Paul,' Ken said abruptly. 'I have.'

A muscle twitched involuntarily at the side of Paul's face. When he spoke there was a strain of desperation in his voice.

'Just let me say this thing,' Paul said. 'Then I won't speak of it again. Perhaps I was wrong to believe all my dream. Perhaps what we have is enough. Remember what you said last night? "I'm on a different track," you said. Well ... *es ist ganz wahr*. Maybe we are on different tracks. But the track can still run side by side.'

Paul stared down at the sand. His hands were clenched so tightly together that the veins seemed to be about to burst through the skin. His fingers twisted nervously together.

Slowly Ken turned and stared at Paul.

'Do you understand now?' Paul asked softly.

Slowly Ken nodded his head.

'So please remember,' Paul concluded.

'That brew must be ready by now,' Ken said.

'Right,' Paul acknowledged, pouring tea and handing a mug to Ken.

'Ta,' Ken said, sipping from the strong, dark liquid.

'I like your plan,' Paul said. 'I do think it is *fabelhaft*. When do you think we could start?'

Ken thought for a moment. 'I see no reason why we shouldn't get under way tonight after sunset.'

'Tonight?'

'The sky would be clear,' Ken explained. 'We could go by the stars. And if it clouds over, we could use the compass. We could only travel by night. By day we'll have to hide up and sleep, because we couldn't risk being seen by either side.'

Paul nodded in agreement. 'And travelling by night it will be cool,' he said. 'We shall need less water. How far shall we have to go?'

'Till we find a tribe of Bedouin.'

Paul spoke slowly. 'We have got some food and water for the journey,' he said. 'We have got the stars and the compass. I'll risk it ... because we will be together.'

For a moment they looked at each other in silence. Ken broke the web of tension which had started to spin between them.

'What would you like to eat for breakfast?' he asked. 'Bully beef and biscuits – or biscuits and bully beef?'

Paul picked up the shovel which was propped against the side of the tank.

'I'll have biscuits and bully beef,' he said, walking off towards the patch of camel-grass a short distance from the tank.

'Your wish is my command,' Ken said, giving a small bow.

'Don't start breakfast without me,' Paul called out.

Ken collected two tins of bully beef and the tin of biscuits from the bivouac. He found the forks. As he moved about preparing the simple meal he began to hum softly to himself. Slowly he began to sing odd sentences and then burst into full-throated song.

'Oh the eagles they fly high in Mobile.
'Oh the eagles they fly high
'And they shit right in your eye,
'Aren't you glad that you and I aren't in Mobile?
'There is always buckshee water in Mobile.
'There is always buckshee water
'And the Padre's buckshee daughter
'Does far more things than she oughter in Mobile.
'In Mobile ...'

'Ken! Ken!' Paul called out urgently.

Ken stopped singing and peered off in the direction of the patch of camel-grass.

'Hello?' he called.

'Look to the north-west,' Paul shouted. 'There is a cloud of dust.'

Ken hastened over to the canvas chair and picked up the binoculars. Moving back towards the tank, he raised the binoculars to his eyes.

'Stay where you are, Paul,' Ken ordered.

'What is it?'

'It's a truck or a jeep,' Ken answered. 'It's coming towards us.'

'Whose side is it?'

'Mine. Get your head down for God's sake, stay out of sight.'

'Ken ...'

'Whatever happens, let me handle this. Stay in the cover of the camel grass,' Ken called out softly. 'Lie still for Christ's sake and don't move.'

Ken scuttled quickly away from the tank. He tossed the binoculars onto the seat of the canvas chair and threw himself into the bivouac. He hurriedly crawled into the sleeping bag.

The sound of the approaching jeep came closer. Then the engine stopped. Suddenly the silence seemed enormous and menacing. Ken lay panting in the sleeping bag. He heard the sound of the door of the jeep slamming shut. He closed his eyes, feigning sleep.

A dark, sensually handsome man of about thirty-five, with a thin, neatly clipped moustache appeared around the side of the tank. On his carefully pressed bush shirt, above the left breast, was the ribbon of the Military Cross. There were three stars on his epaulette showing that he was a captain. A revolver hung from the holster on his webbing belt and his right hand casually rested on it.

'Anyone about?' the man called, moving cautiously towards the bivouac.

Ken opened his eyes and slowly sat up. He stared at the approaching figure noting the cleanness of his trousers and his suede desert boots. Ken wondered how long this immaculate figure had been in the Western Desert. He decided he must either be a comparative newcomer – or he had a very good batman.

As the officer spotted Ken, he drew his revolver.

'You. Get up,' the Captain demanded.

Ken jumped up.

'Are you English?' the man demanded.

'Yes.'

The man smiled and lowered his revolver.

'When I spotted this tank, I never expected to find anyone here.'

'I've been here since our tank brewed up,' Ken explained.

'Oh ...'

'Last week,' Ken continued. 'It got a direct hit.'

The captain peered down at the tracks of the tank.

'Not this tank,' Ken said. 'We were up north.'

The man nodded. 'So you were in that unlucky patrol-in-force that was sent out?'

'Yes.'

'Your lot had a pretty rough time of it by all accounts,' the man said. 'What about you? Is there anything you need? Water? Food? Anything? I've got plenty of stuff on my truck.'

'Nothing, thanks,' Ken said. 'Except if you've got a roll of bandage I could do with a fresh one.'

'What's your name?'

'Preston,' Ken replied.

'My name's Johnson. I'm pretty new to the desert.'

Johnson held out his hand to Ken.

'What's your rank?'

'Trooper,' Ken answered.

'And what is your unit?'

'Hartland Yeomanry.'

'And in the Hartland Yeomanry – troopers don't address a Captain as "Sir"?' Johnson asked, giving a little smile to keep the sting out of his words.

'Yes, they do, sir,' Ken replied.

'Good. Perhaps I had better see your identity disc.'

Ken removed the identity disc which hung around his neck from a thin cord. He passed it across to Johnson, who took it and examined it closely.

'Thanks,' Johnson said, handing the disc back to Ken. 'Was your whole outfit up there in the north?'

'No, sir,' Ken replied. 'Our troop – that's number four troop B. Squadron, sir – were part of the composite squadron that made up the patrol-in-force.'

The Captain thought for a moment. He ran a hand over his face.

'And B Squadron ran into pretty bad trouble quite early on?'

'Yes, sir,' Ken answered. 'It was a proper mix-up. Mr Carey – he's our troop leader, sir – Mr Carey tried to break out south. But we were surrounded. We'd lost two of our tanks already. Then a shell hit our tank, so we baled out.'

'What happened to the rest of your crew?'

'They were killed when the shell hit us,' Ken told him.

Captain Johnson looked slowly around him at the litter of equipment on the sand.

'I'm sorry,' he said, 'but you've not been alone here, have you?'

'No, sir,' Ken replied.

'Where's the other man?' Johnson asked.

For an instant Ken hesitated. 'I was in Mr Carey's tank, sir,' he explained, his mind racing as he worked out his story. 'We were the only two that got out.'

'And where is Mr Carey?'

'He *was* here, sir.'

A look of impatience crossed the Captain's face.

'I can see that,' Johnson said. 'Where is he now? That's what I'm asking you.'

'He left ... He left before first light this morning.'

'Why?' Johnson asked.

'We were running out of food and water. He went to get help.'

'You didn't go with him?'

'Getting out of the driver's hatch,' Ken explained, 'when the tank was burning, I hurt my leg. I think my left tendon's gone.'

'Your tendon as well as the wound in your arm?' Johnson asked. 'Bad luck.'

Ken smiled weakly at the Captain. 'I'll live, sir,' he mumbled.

Johnson opened his map case. 'Mr Carey had his compass, I presume?'

'Yes, sir.'

'What bearing did he leave on this morning?'

For a moment Ken looked confused.

'Well, when Mr Carey left you at first light he must have

given you the bearing he was taking,' Johnson said.

'Yes, sir.'

'Then what was it?'

'Ninety, sir.'

'Due east, in fact?'

'Yes, sir.'

Captain Johnson peered into the bivouac. Then he turned back to face Ken.

'And I see you make use of his sleeping bag while he's away.'

Suddenly Ken felt sweat trickling down his back. Yet it was not sweat caused by the heat of the day; he was sweating because he was nervous. The palms of his hands seemed to be wringing wet; but he was not warm. Ken felt distinctly chilled. However, he realised that at no costs must he allow his nervousness to show.

'Yes, sir,' Ken admitted.

'What time did Mr Carey leave this morning?' Johnson asked.

'Six – no, I'm sorry sir,' Ken answered, 'it must have been nearer five a.m.'

'He left at five,' Johnson said. 'And it is now almost ten. So say with this going he covers ... Yes ... Well, it looks to me as if he's going to be all right – because by now with any luck he'll be in sight of Second Task Force that's regrouping ... I'm on the way there myself. He'd got binoculars with him, I take it?'

'Oh yes, sir.'

'Did he take a haversack?'

Ken nodded. 'Yes, sir.'

'What was his plan?'

'He was going to get a truck and come back for me, sir.'

Each time he spoke, Ken became more aware that Paul was lying in the patch of camel-grass no more than a few yards away. He knew that if Captain Johnson spotted Paul, it was all over. Paul would be taken prisoner – and they would be unable to put their plan into operation.

'Right,' Johnson said, smiling affably at Ken. 'Why don't you gather up your gear and I'll drive you over to Second Task Force.'

Ken drew in a deep breath. He looked down at his hands and was surprised to see that they were without so much as a tremor.

'Mr Carey's orders were for me to wait for him, sir,' he announced firmly.

'But surely now I've arrived the whole situation's changed,' Johnson said.

'Has it, sir?'

'Obviously,' said Johnson. 'I can drive you to Task Force in my jeep, and you can join Mr Carey there.'

'He might have left to come back here before we arrived.'

'Then we'd meet him on the way.'

'No, sir.'

'We'd be on the same bearing,' Johnson pointed out. 'We'd be certain to meet him.'

'Not in this stretch of desert – if you'll excuse me, sir,' Ken argued. 'He could pass us by at a thousand yards and we could miss him. I'm sorry, sir. But I think I'd do best to obey Mr Carey's orders.'

Johnson sighed. 'Very well,' he said. 'I'll leave you some stuff off my jeep before I go.'

'Thank you, sir.'

Johnson gave a nod of acknowledgement. For a moment he gazed silently around at the makeshift camp. He brushed down his neat moustache in what seemed to be an instinctive nervous gesture. Small beads of sweat ran down the sides of his face. When next he spoke he appeared to be far more relaxed and friendly.

'I must say – you've made yourself pretty comfortable here,' he said. 'But then I suppose that's half the business of being a true desert-rat.'

Johnson moved across to the billycan and shook it.

'Water,' he said. 'Got any tea? If not there's some on my jeep.'

'That's okay, sir,' Ken told him. 'I found some tea.'

Johnson smiled at Ken. 'Then why don't we have a brew up?' he asked. 'I can easily let you have another can of water.'

'Right, sir. Shall I make a cup for your driver?'

'Our Colonel's driver went down with gippy tummy this morning,' Johnson explained. 'So the old man has taken mine. I'm doing my own driving.'

Ken nodded.

'I'll get you that can of water,' Johnson said, walking off to his jeep.

Ken began to fiddle with the primus, making the preparations for the tea. Johnson reappeared, carrying a can of water which he placed in the shade at the side of the tank.

'There you are,' Johnson said. 'You know this desert-rat existence is all new to me ... I'm fresh out from England. I've only been in the Western Desert a month. So I don't really know the form yet ... But that's what I've been swanning around with the Long Range Desert Group to find out ... My main job now is to find out what makes our desert army tick, what makes it work ... For the time being my fighting days are over ... I had my share of excitement on the way back to Dunkirk.'

'And won yourself a medal into the bargain, sir,' Ken said. 'So I see.'

'I don't mean I didn't fire off a gun this last week or so,' Johnson continued. 'I did.'

Johnson produced a cigarette case and extended it towards Ken.

'But I'm no longer concerned with the enemy as such. I'm concerned with the troops that are fighting him. Cigarette?'

'Ta,' Ken said, taking one from the proffered case. 'Much appreciated, sir.'

'You've got a light?'

'Yes, sir. Thank you.'

'I've talked with some of the men in the Long Range Desert Group during my fortnight with them ... How's that tea coming along?'

'Sorry, sir. Excuse me,' Ken said, peering at the water to see if it was boiling.

'But I intended anyhow to meet some of the infantry and some of the tank crew men,' Johnson continued. 'So you see, Preston, I'm really glad to have this opportunity of chatting to you. Now you're not a regular, are you?'

Ken shook his head. 'No, sir,'

'Well, I am,' Johnson said, warming to his subject. 'I was a sergeant six years ago. I came up the hard way – as the bishop said to the chorus girl.'

Ken gave a faint grin.

Johnson lowered himself into the canvas chair.

'How long have you been out here, Preston?'

'Two years, sir.'

'Two years! Well, you must have seen quite a bit of the Bengazi Handicap, as we call it … Do rest that leg of yours.'

'Thank you, sir,' Ken said, sitting down on the upturned ammunition box. He reminded himself that he must remember to limp.

'Who do you and your friends reckon is the best General out here in the Western Desert?' Johnson asked casually. 'The best general on either side …'

Ken thought for a moment. 'I suppose Rommel, sir.'

'Exactly. That is precisely the answer I expected. In fact, an Army Order has recently been circulated to all troop-leaders to the effect that – and I quote – "This adulation of General Rommel must cease." But that's not the right way about it. Now, what do *you* admire so much about Rommel?'

Ken was silent.

'Well,' Johnson said, prompting him, 'I daresay you heard the story that Rommel visited a Field Hospital his troops had over-run and talked to every wounded British soldier in it?'

'Yes, sir,' Ken agreed.

'I thought so. Well, the story is perfectly true so far as it goes. He talked to almost each one of our men – asking him if he was being properly treated and so on. But what you probably don't know is that Rommel had already made his plans to withdraw the following day. So he knew, you see, that every man in that hospital would get back to his unit and the story would spread all over the Eighth Army. Brilliant propaganda for them, you see?'

Johnson lowered his head and inclined himself forward in the chair as if he were about to impart some especial piece of wisdom to Ken.

'Well, now *we're* going to organise some propaganda,' he announced. 'For a British General for a change. And every soldier in the Eighth Army will be taught to appreciate that the Afrika Korps is made up of Nazis. They are Nazis to a man – Rommel included. And the Nazis ... Well, your outfit didn't fight in France, did it?'

'No, sir.'

'I was an Intelligence Officer and I've seen some of their work. It's not very pretty.'

'Excuse me, sir,' Ken said, measuring tea into the two mugs.

'Carry on,' Johnson said. 'But out here in the desert a strange kind of camaraderie has grown up between the two sides, hasn't it.'

'You could say that,' Ken agreed. 'Yes, sir.'

'Well, it's going to stop – and pretty damn quick,' Johnson said emphatically. 'I'm tired of hearing about the chivalry of the enemy. We've got to stop all this silly talk about the poor Italian soldier who doesn't want to fight us at all.'

Johnson paused and shook his head. He watched silently as Ken prepared the mugs of tea.

'You probably know the answer to that one,' he continued. 'It's the Italians who started the fighting out here – and they're still in the field. Whether he likes it or not, every officer and every enlisted man in the Eighth Army must understand that he's been sent out to this Godforsaken desert for one reason and for one reason only – to destroy the enemy by every possible means.'

Johnson smiled as if in apology for his serious, rather hectoring tone of voice.

'What's the name of your Colonel?' he asked.

'Colonel Parmenter, sir.'

'Parmenter? Didn't he win himself a DSO in the winter campaign?'

'Yes, sir. That's right.'

Ken was about to add sugar to Johnson's mug of tea.

'No sugar for me, thanks,' Johnson said.

'Right, sir,' Ken said, handing the mug of tea to the Captain.

'What are you?' Johnson asked. 'A gunner?'

'Driver, sir.'

'Your regiment has got Crusaders, I presume?'

'Yes, sir.'

'What do you think of the new Crusader Mark Six?'

'The engine's fine, sir,' Ken told him. 'But the cooling-system could certainly do with some improvement. It's the gun that's the trouble.'

'Why?'

'The two-pounder's not big enough,' Ken explained.

'Quite … Well, it's being put right.'

'If they gave us a bigger gun, there'd be no complaints.'

' "They",' Johnson repeated. 'Who is this "they"?'

Ken stared at him blankly.

'Well …?'

'The people in England who send the stuff out here, I suppose, sir.'

Johnson shook his head. 'No, Preston, there's no "they",' he said sharply. 'There's no "we" and there's no "they". We're all fighting in the same army, against the same enemy.'

'Yes, sir.'

Johnson heaved himself out of the canvas chair and wandered over to Paul's bivouac. Noticing the paperback on the sand, he picked it up and examined the cover.

'What's this?' he asked. 'Were you reading it?'

'Yes, sir.'

'To hear them talk about the Eighth Army at home you'd imagine that every man was reading Jane Austen or *War and Peace*.'

Johnson flicked through a few pages of the book. '*The*

Crimson Moll,' he said. 'Quite a good title. It sounds like a really juicy read.'

'Another cup of tea, sir?' Ken asked, trying desperately to get Johnson away from the bivouac.

Johnson turned back to the bivouac. He picked up the mouth-organ and examined it.

'No thank you, Preston,' he said, continuing to examine the mouth-organ. 'Made in Germany, I see.'

'Yes, sir,' Ken answered. 'I got it off a Jerry tank we captured in the winter campaign.'

Nervously, Ken began to clear away the tea and sugar.

'I see,' Johnson said.

'We get quite a bit of loot that way,' Ken told him.

'Loot?'

Johnson picked up a forage cap from the bivouac. He then examined the pillow at the head of the sleeping bag, the shoes and the shirt. As he examined the shirt he discovered a wallet in the breast pocket. He stood up, putting the wallet in his own pocket, and left the bivouac.

'Yes, sir,' Ken said. 'You never know when extra clothes will come in useful. Gets a bit cold out here at night. We collect all the stuff we can. Last campaign I did fine. I got two cameras and a whacking great pair of binoculars ... not to mention a fur-lined jacket. Then my tank brewed up and I lost the bleeding lot, and me own clobber as well. One thing that the Jerries have that we don't – chocolate – bags of the stuff. Ever taste some, sir? Delicious. It's got special vitamins added, or so they say. All I can tell you for certain is that if you eat too much you'll be sick as a dog.'

Johnson raised his hand as if to silence Ken. He walked across to the tank and climbed onto it. He raised his binoculars to his eyes and scanned the ground to the west. Then he lowered the binoculars and jumped from the tank and moved closer towards Ken.

'I thought I heard a convoy,' he said. 'But it's nothing.'

Johnson smoothed down his bush shirt. 'Preston, I rather think I met your troop-leader, Mr Carey, at a Corps Exercise back in England,' he said suddenly. 'Isn't he a rather thin, fair-haired man?'

Ken shook his head. 'He's thin, all right. But he's dark,' he replied. 'Very dark, I'd say.'

'Then it can't be the same chap.'

Johnson picked up the shirt and the mouth-organ for a second time and stared at them contemplatively for a while. He raised his gaze and directed it towards Ken.

"All enemy loot?' he asked.

'Yes, sir ...'

Johnson took the wallet from his shirt pocket.

Ken kicked the sand at his feet in agitation, then he controlled himself.

'Including this?' Johnson said, holding up the wallet.

'Yes, sir.'

'You found this wallet on a Jerry tank?'

'Yes, sir. A Mark Four.'

Johnson sat down in the canvas chair. With a calculated movement, he slapped the wallet up and down on the palm of his hand while, all the time, watching Ken's reactions.

'Your regiment got as far as Agedabia, didn't it?' he asked. 'On the last advance?'

'Yes, sir.'

'When was that, roughly?'

'January, sir.'

'And when did the withdrawal begin?'

'January the twenty-first, I think, sir.'

'So, when did you capture the Mark Four?'

'Mid-January, sir.'

'And that's when you found this wallet?'

'Yes, sir.'

Slowly Johnson pulled a letter out of the wallet and stared at it intently. He raised his eyes and gazed at Ken. The expression on his face had now become impassive.

'Then how do you explain the fact that this letter from Germany and written in German – which I understand – is post-marked February sixteenth? How do you explain that, Preston?' Johnson demanded.

'There must be some mistake, sir.'

'I hope for your sake there is.'

'I don't quite understand the meaning of that remark, sir.'

'Come here, Preston ...' Johnson ordered.

Ken walked slowly forward.

'I'm now forced to ask you some questions,' Johnson stated. 'I have to warn you that if it turns out that you lie to me in answer you will automatically be put on a charge. Is that clear, Preston?'

'Yes, sir.'

'Where is your troop-leader?'

'I told you, sir. He left an hour before first light.'

'Who slept in that sleeping-bag last night?'

'Mr Carey.'

'Alone?'

'Yes, sir.'

'Where did you sleep?'

'There sir,' Ken said, pointing to his rough bivouac beside the tank.

'When did you move across to the sleeping-bag?'

'After Mr Carey left, sir.'

'When he left, you say?'

Ken nodded. 'Yes, sir.'

'But at five this morning, it must have still been very cold?'

'Yes, sir.'

'So did you get into the sleeping bag?'

Ken stepped forward a few paces and stood smartly to attention in front of Johnson.

'Sir,' he asked, 'sir, can I ask what all this is about?'

Johnson ignored the question.

'Mr Carey's a fair-haired man, you say?'

'Yes, sir. No. He's dark, sir.'

'You told me you'd read that book. The paperback.'

'Yes, sir.'

'What was the name of the girl in it? The crimson moll, what's her name?'

Ken hesitated. 'I only skimmed through it, sir. I'm not one for much reading. I can't remember.'

'Was it Jill or Dana or Marilyn?'

'It was one of them. I'm sure of it.'

Johnson remained silent for a moment. He glared at Ken. 'No it wasn't, Preston. It wasn't any of them,' he said in a cold voice. 'I presume that during your two years out here in the desert you've learned the Army regulations with regards to prisoners of war?'

'Yes, sir.'

'And you do know therefore that it's a serious offence to assist the enemy in any way?'

'Yes, sir.'

'How long have you been here?'

'Three days.'

'With Mr Carey?'

'Yes, sir.'

Johnson stroked his moustache thoughtfully. 'No one else has been here?' he asked.

'I know what it is – at least, I think I do, sir,' Ken said. 'You've seen all this equipment lying about, so you think there's been a Jerry soldier here.'

'Am I wrong?'

Ken gazed straight at Johnson. 'No, sir. You're right. There was two of them, here. Their tank brewed up, and they got badly wounded. Then they got lost. Then they found this tank. A day later one of them died ... And when me and Mr Carey arrived, the second one was dying. We buried him two days ago. You may have seen the two graves as you drove here, sir.'

'No, I don't believe I did.'

Johnson stood up. He picked up the binoculars and walked over to the tank. He scrambled on top of it and looked out to the west and then to the north.

'To the north, sir. More to the north,' Ken directed him.

'Oh, yes ... I see. Two graves – side by side. That's what you mean, isn't it?'

'Yes, sir.'

'Those were the graves you dug?'

'Yes. I dug them, sir.'

'All right, Preston. Quite.'

Johnson jumped down from the tank and walked back towards Ken.

'I'll give you one last chance to tell the truth,' he said.

'I've told you the truth, sir,' Ken replied.

'I don't think so,' Johnson declared firmly. 'So let me tell you, Preston, that when I first climbed onto the tank a few minutes ago, I was particularly interested in the ground lying to the west – where there's a stretch of camel-grass. Is there anything you want to say to me?'

Ken shook his head, 'No, sir,' he said.

'As I examined that area I came across a patch where there was something which attracted my attention. So I focussed more closely on it. And I found it was a man. He was lying face downwards in the sand. He wasn't moving. He had fair hair. You haven't seen such a man, have you, Preston?'

'No, sir.'

'There's been no German anywhere near this tank today?'

'I've told you, no, sir.'

'Perhaps he wasn't a Jerry,' Johnson said. 'He was certainly fair-haired. He was very blond, I'd reckon. I say "was" because he's gone. When I was up on the tank a minute ago there was no sign of him.'

Johnson looked at Ken as if expecting him to speak. But Ken remained silent. Johnson shook his head.

'But he won't get far,' he continued. 'I'm considered a pretty good shot. Last week, for instance, I started up a hare in a stretch of camel-grass down south. So I gave chase in the truck. And I shot it dead at twenty yards.'

'I'm sorry, sir,' Ken said quietly. 'But I still don't understand what all this is about.'

'Shall I tell you something, Preston?' Johnson said. 'Semi-educated, semi-clever people always make the same mistake. They always underrate the intelligence of the person they're dealing with. So, let's consider the facts, shall we? You've obviously helped the man. You've given him shelter. You've lied for him. You've got yourself into serious trouble for his sake. So apparently you must have become friends with him.

For what reason I cannot imagine. But do you think that counts for anything so far as he's concerned? No! He's concerned with one thing – and one thing only – to save his skin. So that while we've been talking here, that's what he's been planning. Because, of course, all this time my jeep has been standing there unguarded – as you've seen for yourself – in the dead ground below the ridge.'

From his trouser pocket Johnson took a small bakelite object.

'You know what this is?' he asked.

'A Rotor arm, sir,' Ken replied.

'*And* I've got the keys,' Johnson added. 'So he's hardly likely to start the engine. But we'll hear him open the jeep door. And when he discovers he hasn't got a chance, he'll creep off below that ridge and head south. He'll make a run for it. That will be when the chase begins.'

Ken stared hard at Johnson, an expression of dismay on his face.

'I'm not strict on discipline,' Johnson continued. 'I never have been – and the very last thing I want is any fuss or trouble. But this kind of thing is a disease. Because like a disease it can spread. It can sap the whole morale of an army.'

Ken continued to stare silently at Johnson.

'I wonder what you're thinking,' Johnson said quietly.

'I'm thinking, sir, that you've got things wrong,' Ken replied.

'How? How have I? Tell me, Preston?'

'I don't know Army Regulations, and you do, sir,' Ken said. 'That's obvious. So perhaps you can tell me ... Supposing there had been a Jerry soldier here, and supposing he'd been sick and I'd looked after him, would I have been breaking any regulations?'

'If he'd been your prisoner, and he'd been wounded or sick and you'd looked after him? No, I don't think so. But – as I'm sure you're intelligent enough to realise – there are other offences you'll be charged with?'

'Offences, sir?'

'Helping an enemy, for one.'

'They'd have to prove that, wouldn't they?'

'There would be my testimony,' Johnson said. 'This whole charade we've just been through shows that you've been aiding him. But that's one of the reasons why I intend to make sure that I catch your friend. I shall be most surprised if he doesn't talk. After all, what will he have to lose?'

For an instant, Ken looked at Johnson with an expression of open dislike and contempt. Then he resumed his impassive gaze. But Johnson had not missed the quick flicker of emotion on Ken's face.

'You're still very confident,' he said. 'Aren't you? Obviously you don't believe he'll talk. But then, of course, you don't think he'll desert you now, do you? I wonder what has made you behave with such criminal idiocy. I must confess that I can't understand it. I don't understand what makes you tick. And I ought to be able to.'

Johnson suddenly turned away and began to walk towards his jeep. Ken made as if to shout out – and at that moment Johnson turned abruptly back to face him.

'Why didn't you call out to him, I wonder?' he asked. 'You were just about to – weren't you? Surely you don't think he's got a chance? I must confess it – I simply do not understand you.'

'Nor ever you will,' Ken said in a flat voice.

'Perhaps not,' Johnson answered. 'Well, in a minute or two we can safely assume that he's discovered he can't use the jeep. So then he'll head south. But so as to make sure, I intend to give him five minutes' start.'

Johnson watched the expression of Ken's face. The heavy silence closed oppressively about them.

'Sir,' Ken said suddenly. 'I've changed my mind ...'

'Oh yes?' Johnson replied casually.

'I'll tell the truth ... I'll make a statement and sign it – if that's what you want, sir. But ...'

'But what?'

'He's just a trooper – like I am. He's just one of thousands ... Just one of us can't make a twopenny bit of difference to the war ... No more than a grain of sand in the desert can make any difference, sir. So please, can't you let him go?'

'I say it again. I can't understand you, Preston. The man would quite obviously desert you. Yet you're perfectly prepared to get yourself shut up in a military prison for at least a year. And why? In order to spare him being sent to a prisoner-of-war camp? He'd probably be far better off there than fighting in this desert. So why do you want me to let him go? Tell me why, Preston.'

Ken spoke very quietly. 'So he doesn't have to be interrogated, sir.'

'Perhaps I do begin to understand you ... You don't want all the other prisoners in his camp to know about him.'

'Sir, if I tell the truth,' Ken said, 'sir, if I sign the statement ...'

But Johnson was no longer listening to him. He was looking away to the west. He turned back to face Ken.

'But the situation now doesn't arise ...' he said.

Ken looked past Johnson and saw why everything had suddenly changed. Dispiritedly, Paul was walking back towards the makeshift camp. He walked slowly closer, and on his face there was an expression of utter defeat. As he drew close to where Johnson and Ken were standing, Paul stopped. He tried to smile at Ken; then his gaze flickered towards Johnson.

'You couldn't start the jeep, could you? But I wonder why you came back. We'll find that out presently. But first – let's have your name, rank and number.'

Paul remained standing forlornly silent.

'Come on,' Johnson snapped impatiently. 'I know you speak English, so don't bother to pretend you can't understand me. I want your name, rank and number. *Verstehen Sie?*'

Paul glanced back towards Ken, who gave a slight nod.

'Seidler. *Gemeiner Panzarsoldat. Zweihundertfünfundvierzig. Acht vier sechs sieben.*'

'How long have you been here?'

Again Paul glanced towards Ken.

'Doesn't matter,' Ken said. 'Tell him.'

'Six days.'

'So you were here before Preston arrived?'

'Yes.'

'And you were here three days together?'

'Yes.'

'Where did you sleep?'

Paul still had not understood the drift of Johnson's questions. He pointed towards the bivouac.

'There,' he said.

'Show me,' Johnson ordered.

Paul walked across to the bivouac with Johnson following him.

'There,' Paul repeated, pointing at the sleeping-bag.

'In the sleeping-bag?'

'Yes,' Paul answered.

Ken's face was now distorted with worry as he desperately tried to think of some way of escaping from the trap. Johnson turned towards Ken.

'And *where* did you sleep, Preston?' he asked.

Ken pointed to his makeshift bivouac at the side of the tank. 'I slept there, sir,' he said. 'I made it up when I arrived here.'

The expression on Johnson's face was now stern.

'But you told me that when Mr Carey left you slept in that bivouac in the sleeping bag. And there's only one sleeping bag. I must tell you, Preston, that I don't believe a single word you've said. I don't believe Mr Carey was ever anywhere near this tank. But your German friend *did* sleep in that sleeping-bag – because earlier I found a strand of fair hair on the pillow and you had told me that Mr Carey had dark hair. So that was your first lie. I'm sure the rest of the evidence won't be hard to get.'

Paul turned towards Ken. He looked confused. 'What does he mean?' he asked. 'What is this evidence he talks about?'

'He means that he's making various charges against me,' Ken answered grimly. 'He means that he'll get me sent to the glass-house.'

Paul nodded to show that he had understood. He edged closer to Ken and spoke to him in a whisper.

'The jeep is no good,' he said. 'He's taken the key.'

Johnson looked at Paul. 'Precisely,' he said.

Paul's eyes were still fixed on Ken.

'I thought that if I could move the jeep,' he said, 'then you ...'

'But he's got the keys and the rotor arm – and a gun,' Ken said, interrupting him quickly.

'I wonder what you were afraid he was going to blurt out then?' Johnson asked Ken.

Ken ignored Johnson. 'We're not beaten yet,' he said to Paul.

Johnson stiffened. 'Do you now range yourself on the enemy's side?' he asked in a cold voice. 'I'm asking you. Do you, Preston?'

Ken hesitated. He nodded his head slowly. 'Yes,' he said. 'I do.'

'Realising the crime and its consequences,' Johnson shouted as the anger mounted in him. 'You take the side of the enemy against me? Do you? Do you?'

'Yes,' Ken answered quietly.

'Very well, I shall treat you accordingly. So you know where you stand. But I don't think you'll be quite so sure of your decision after a few months in the glass-house – let alone a few years. I've seen far better men than you broken down – and far stronger.'

As he spoke, Johnson removed the revolver from his holster.

'They won't break me down,' Ken said.

'I'll give them three months,' Johnson told him.

'They won't break me down, because they won't get the chance.'

'They will, Preston,' Johnson said. 'I can assure you of it.'

'Yes, I'm sure you can ... Your type's always existed, you always will. And it's when I hear you and your lot talking that I know what my "kind" as you call us is really fighting against.'

'The jeep won't do you much good,' Johnson announced.

Ken glanced around, then he moved quickly towards the dune and the jeep.

'No,' he said savagely. 'But I can make sure that you won't start it either.'

Ken moved further towards the jeep.

'If you move one more step, I'll kill you,' Johnson declared. 'Don't be a fool. If you sabotage the jeep it won't do you any good.'

Ken stood still. Johnson took half-a-dozen steps after him and raised the revolver so that it pointed directly at him.

'We'll see,' Ken said, and continued to walk towards the jeep.

'Preston, stop,' Johnson called. 'I'm giving you twenty more paces ... Twenty, Preston. One, two , three, four, five, six, seven, eight, nine ...'

As Johnson slowly counted off the paces, his complete attention was directed towards the receding figure of Ken. For an instant Paul remained utterly still, listening in horror as Johnson continued to count off the numbers. Then, with an agile movement, he slipped towards the bivouac. As he opened the lid of the dixie there was a sharp click.

Johnson swivelled around to see Paul taking out the revolver and raising it towards him. Without a moment's hesitation Johnson fired at Paul. A cloud of cordite filled the air; with a cry of pain Paul spun round and fell in front of the bivouac.

Johnson rushed forward and snatched up the gun which had fallen from Paul's fingers into the sand.

Ken ran back to the tank. He stood still for a moment, panting for breath. Then he hurried across the narrow strip of sand to Paul and, kneeling, propped up his head with the pillow from the sleeping-bag. Blood pumped from a gaping wound at the left side of Paul's chest.

'You treacherous little bastard,' Johnson shouted at Ken. 'You knew that gun was there. You'd have let an officer of your own side be murdered in cold blood.'

Ken raised his head and glared across at Johnson. His eyes

were filled with hatred. 'He's dying,' he blurted out. 'You fucking bastard. You've killed him.'

Paul wheezed for breath. Blood continued to pour from the wound.

'*Entschuldigen Sie,*' he gasped with difficulty. 'I was slow ... I ought to have moved more fast ... *Entschuldigen* ... I'm sorry, Ken.'

'It makes me sick,' Johnson said furiously. 'You don't even know what we're out here for.'

'I'm sorry, Ken ...' Paul muttered.

'With him you hadn't much chance ...' Ken told him gently.

'What do you think gives you the right to make a truce of your own,' Johnson demanded angrily. 'When I think we're supposed to be at war – you're not fit to run a kindergarten, let alone a country.'

'Lie still,' Ken said softly to Paul. 'You must let me dress your wound.'

'All along,' Paul whispered, 'all along I hadn't much chance.' He tried to raise himself but fell back on the pillow. 'Then three days ago – my luck changed.'

'There's no luck and there's no chance,' Ken said bitterly.

Johnson carefully replaced the revolver in his holster. 'Preston,' he said in a voice of command. 'I've got the precise map reference. So you can expect them to come back for you in about two hours. I must warn you – it won't do you much good trying to escape. You won't get anywhere in two hours. Understood?'

Ken ignored Johnson. He was dimly aware that the Captain was moving away from the tank towards the jeep. For a moment the only sound was Paul's hoarse breathing, then he heard the sound of the engine starting. For an instant the engine roared, then it kicked into life. Slowly the sound of the jeep faded away.

'Ken ...' Paul cried out weakly. 'Ken ...'

'It's all right. I'm here.'

Paul stirred, his face a mask of pain. 'Do you think there is anything?' he asked.

'After this lot – there'd better be.'

'When you've closed your eyes ...' Paul began, 'for the last time ...'

A spasm of pain stopped Paul from speaking any further. Ken placed an arm round Paul and held him gently.

'I can hear it ...' Paul continued, struggling for breath. 'I can hear it so clear ... And it doesn't matter any more – *Es macht gar nichts* – because we found it, didn't we?'

'Yes,' Ken muttered.

'Say it, Ken, please. Say the words.'

'We found it,' Ken said clearly.

'It will be sad ... alone again. Ken ... don't let them ...'

Paul fell back on the pillow. A thin trickle of blood escaped from the corner of his mouth and ran down his chin. The blood from the wound continued to spill out onto the sand of the desert.

*

Circling high above the shifting sands of the desert was a hawk. Through a hard, dark eye it saw the movements of men down below. The bird wheeled gracefully higher and higher in the clear blue sky until the size of the men had so diminished that they appeared no larger than ants toiling on the infinite sand, making actions without meaning and which could affect no one.

Author's Note

The incident which forms the central theme of *Enemy* (the meeting between an English and a German soldier) is based upon an event which happened to me almost forty years ago while I was fighting in the war in the Western Desert. I make a brief reference to this meeting in my book about those experiences, *Come to Dust* (published in 1945).

I wrote a play based upon that episode. *Enemy*, for that was the title, was staged in London in 1969. Yet my meeting, during a battle which was still raging, with a young German officer whose tank had been destroyed still haunted me.

My friend Peter Burton suggested that this strange desert meeting – when neither the German nor I knew who would win the battle nor who, at the end of the day, would be the prisoner and who the captor – might form the basis for a novel. This is the genesis of the present work.

I should like to stress, however, that the novel *Enemy* is a completely new work which has used the characters and essential plot of the play but which contains a mass of new material – both by way of characters and incidents. I should also like to make clear that though the central theme stems from an incident taken from my life, none of the characters in the book is meant to represent any person living or dead – except in the instances where I have used the names of historical personages.

Enemy would not have been written without Peter Burton's help – and I am extremely grateful for all his assistance with the research, planning and writing of the book.

Robin Maugham
Brighton

Millivres Books can be ordered from any bookshop in the UK and from specialist bookshops overseas. If you prefer to order by mail, please send the full retain price and 80p (UK) or £2 (overseas) per title for postage and packing to:

Dept MBKS
Millivres Ltd
Ground Floor
Worldwide House
116–134 Bayham Street
London NW1 0BA

A comprehensive catalogue is available on request.